# *Willow Run*

# Willow Run
## Copyright 1999 by Frost Publishing

## FROST PUBLISHING

Winter Park, Florida 32789

Printed in the United States of America
First Edition

Edited by Anne Frost
Cover Photography by Linda Neff

Lynch, James R.
Willow Run ,
1. Title 1999 ISBN: 1-888422-53-X

# Other Books by James R. Lynch

## Jimmy Boy

Copyright 1990

ISBN: 0-9614624-7-7
Frost Publishing
Winter Park, Florida
Printed in the United States of America

## Checkmate

Copyright 1996

ISBN: 0-9614624-5-5
Frost Publishing
Winter Park, Florida
Printed in the United States of America

## Dedication

This book is dedicated to all those who have had to live in areas with bad streams from mines that poison the water and with foul air from the mines. It is also dedicated to every woman who needs a visit from the Kinch brothers. Last but not least, to all the children who have a male in their lives who confuses brutality with being a man.

## Acknowledgement

Writing a book to me is fun. Probably because I pay little attention to grammar. Editing my work must be quite a challenge. I know this and feel a certain amount of guilt in just asking someone to do it. Anne Frost somehow manages to do it and even make it an enjoyable experience. Anne, many thanks for your patience and understanding. I would like to thank my sister, Linda for taking all the photos which are shown in the book. The pictures on the cover of the book are exceptional. I hope she feels the book does her beautiful pictures justice.

# *Chapter One*

The motors on the private plane seemed to sound a little high pitched. No one was paying any attention to them as they boarded the plane.

Ed and Esther Thompson were flying in a private corporate plane from Memphis to Pittsburgh.

Ed and cousin Ben were the last two surviving heirs to a sizable family estate. The estate in essence made them the principal owners of a large major national metals company that had its headquarters based in Pittsburgh.

Both Ben and Ed had agreed to establish a trust which would by-pass their generation and give the bulk of their estate to their children. According to the terms of the trust, the funds would be distributed when the youngest was thirty years old.

At the time they were both in their late twenties. They were both married with one son each. The babies were born just two days apart.

Ed had just received his doctorate in physics. He was looking forward to getting on with he rest of his life.

Ben had dropped out of college in his junior year. He was more the playboy type.

Although the paperwork had been agreed upon and signed, Ed learned that Ben had recently used the plane.

Ben liked the outdoors and he was into mountain climbing in a big way. On occasions they would fly him to some remote place. The crew would stay there and assist him with air drops of supplies. By doing this, at times, they could bypass having to set up base camps.

The day had just faded to black as they boarded the plane. The sun going down had taken the edge off of the sweltering heat on this late August day.

The flight plan on that day, August 25, 1953, listed the travel time at about three hours more or less depending upon the prevailing winds.

The plane lifted off smoothly from the airfield. Gaining some altitude and looking west, one could catch just a trace of color of the day's end.

During the first two hours of the flight everything went smoothly. The co-pilot came back and gave them some beverage. Esther had finished feeding and diapering their two month old son. The plane was loaded and the space was so small and confining that the unpleasant odor of the diaper change could almost bring one to tears.

Out of boredom Ed got up and was moving around in the plane. The interior had just been redecorated and he was admiring the work. In the rear of the plane he found some of Ben's mountain climbing gear. There were some small parachutes stacked up that were used for dropping supplies for him when he was conducting his outdoor activities.

Ed sat back down by Esther. They had had little chance to talk since he finished school. They had not even had time to discuss their plans for the future. In the recent past, getting his degree had been a full time goal. Now they could start building their lives together. He loved Esther and he hoped that John would be the first of several children.

Money would never be a problem. With what he had already received in inheritance they would be able to live like royalty for the rest of their lives.

Something jolted the plane. The jolt was similar to having a fender bender in the car.

After the initial impact the plane started shaking. The captain came on and said that one of the engines had blown. He suspected that there might be a problem with the propeller. He said that they were cruising at twenty thousand feet and he would be starting down.

The plane was making a strange whining noise and a short time later, something tore a big hole in the side of the plane. It must have been the propeller breaking loose. When it tore through the plane it cut some of the steering cables and communication lines.

The captain could not call out and he was having trouble keeping the plane in the air. There was panic in everyone's faces.

Having a doctorate in physics, unfortunately, Ed knew what was happening. He knew when the engine had finally seized, the propeller that was running wild would break free.

He gave Esther a hard kiss. He knew what he had to do. He got out of his seat and managed to get to the rear of the plane. Picking up one of the small parachutes he went back to his seat.

The plane was shaking so hard that you had to hang on to something just to get around.

The baby was in a carrying basket. Ed took a blanket and wrapped it completely around the basket. Then he took a second blanket and did the same thing securing the baby firmly inside the basket.

The captain came back again and told them that they were at ten thousand feet and he could not maintain altitude because the second engine was heating up.

Ed continued to work on the basket. He finally managed to tie one of the parachutes to it.

The captain came back again and told them they were at five thousand feet.

The co-pilot managed to stick his head out the door opening to the cockpit and saw what Ed was doing. Ed shouted for him to tell him when they had dropped to three thousand feet.

In just a few minutes, the co-pilot told Ed they were at three thousand feet.

Summing up all of his emotional strength and knowing there was no alternative, Ed tossed the basket and the parachute out the gaping hole in the side of the plane.

Ed managed to make his way back to Esther. He sat next to her. They hugged and they were both crying, not for themselves but for the baby.

The captain came back and said that the second engine had cooled off some and was now working a little better. He didn't think they could land the plane but he felt that they might be able to stay up just a little longer.

Ed and Esther took that time to make their peace with the Lord.

They held on to each other as a large roar and a ball of fire instantly took their lives.

# *Chapter Two*

Hilda Willow was walking down the long dirt road that led from the small town of Franklin to her house. The road was originally used for the coal mines.

The mines had been closed for some time. Still left in the hollow were a few small and older homes. Most of the homes were in very poor condition and empty. All were on their last legs.

The hollow where they lived was formed by two hills that came down sharply to the valley floor. The hollow was split by the creek. It ran down the middle, for the most part, but on occasion moved from one side of the hill to the other. At the narrowest point between the hills there was just enough room for the creek and the road.

Hilda's house was located on one of the wider parts of the hollow. The surrounding area was completely covered with trees of all kinds. Where there had been homes in the past, one could still find some fruit and nut trees. In these areas one was also likely to find patches of raspberries, blueberries and gooseberries. There were wild grapes on the vines in the old growth trees. The entire hollow was conveniently covered with a tall canopy of trees that kept it cool in the summer.

Hilda had made the half mile walk many times. This time it was particularly painful. She was coming from the small clinic in this one doctor town. Barely a week before, she had had a premature delivery. In addition to being premature there were other complications as well. The baby had lived only a short period of time.

Dr. Rhodes, the town doctor, had asked her if she wanted to donate the baby to the state medical school. She thought for awhile, then she agreed. She wasn't thinking about what she wanted to do but what her husband might think and do when he found out.

Hilda was nineteen years old. She already had two sons, Billy who was three and Bobby who was two.

Her husband, Homer, was in the army. He was stationed in Germany. He would be coming home in about eight months. She wasn't looking forward to that. Homer had a mean streak and she wondered how he would take the news of the baby dying. She also wondered how he would react to her giving the baby up to a medical school for research. He had beaten her for less in the past.

Hilda was about two hundred feet from her house when she noticed something in the high briar bushes off to the side of the road. At first she thought it looked strange. As she got closer it looked like someone's sheets had blown off the clothes line. Then she noticed string coming from the fabric to a basket. The basket was wrapped with a blanket. Hearing a noise coming from the basket, she thought there must be some kind of animal inside. She stepped off the road into the briar bushes in the direction of the sound.

Reaching the spot, the blankets were tied securely to the basket. It took her awhile to get everything untied. Before she did, the sounds that she was hearing told her that it was a baby. She gathered up the baby in the basket, the string and fabric and took them to her house.

The baby seemed to be alright but she was not sure. While at home she fed and changed the baby. Then she headed back to the doctor's office.

She still had not regained her strength from her clinic stay. However with the excitement of finding the baby she made good time getting to the clinic.

Doctor Rhodes's clinic was small but it was well suited for a town the size of Franklin. His nurse was on vacation and he was holding down the fort by himself.

Hilda got to the doctor's office during the his lunch break. All of the patients were gone and the office was empty.

Dr. Rhodes was a trim six foot tall man. He was very unpretentious and he treated everyone the same. His life was his work. He sincerely cared for everyone who came to him for help. His hair started turning gray in his twenties. When he was thirty-five years old his hair was completely white. He lost little hair, if any, over the years and he always stood out with that full head of hair. With his fast pace at the clinic he had to learn to take time to talk to his patients. This he had learned well and the patients loved him for it. He had found a place where he was needed. What he did he did to perfection. It was one of those times when things came together right.

As the doctor was checking the baby over she told the doctor how she had found it. He estimated the baby to be two or three months old and in good health.

Hilda and the doctor looked over the clothing and the basket. They were unable to find any identification or any clue of where the baby came from or who left it there. It's sudden appearance remained a mystery.

The thought crossed Hilda's mind that she could keep the baby. She was still full of milk. The nurse was on vacation. The doctor had not told anyone that her baby had died.. She could just keep the baby and no one would know except her and the doctor. Not even Homer, her husband, would know. When she approached the doctor he was not too receptive to the idea. The doctor had known Hilda all of her life. As a matter of fact he had delivered her.

Hilda's folks had died in an auto accident when she was fifteen years old. Shortly after that she married Homer.

Dr. Rhodes thought about the alternative of the child being raised in an orphanage and figured that Hilda's plan might not be so bad after all.

The doctor tried once more to talk her out of it. She had made her mind up. He told Hilda that he had an obligation to find out who the parents of the child were. He said if he found them he would be obligated to notify them. In the mean time she could keep the baby while he looked for its parents.

In a short time Hilda was taking her new son, Jimmy, home. Hilda was walking down that same road but this time she was happy. Just a few hours ago she had felt like dying while coming home after losing her baby.

Hilda was happy but concerned. This two month old baby didn't look like a newborn..

Hilda's friend, Rita, who lived about an hour's drive away had taken the other two boys home with her. She was keeping them while Hilda had her new baby. She called Rita to ask her to keep the boys for a couple weeks. She agreed.

Hilda disposed of everything she had found with the baby. She cut it up and burned it. Then she spread the ashes.

For the first time she took a hard look at the baby. Compared to her two other children, his color was a shade lighter as were his eyes and hair. However she didn't think it enough difference to cause any concern.

The weeks she had at home alone with the baby were some of the most enjoyable of her life. It had given her some time to reflect. She knew she didn't love Homer but she loved the children. She was displeased with where they lived but she saw little chance of things changing.

She bundled up the baby and went outside the house into the yard. The first hint of autumn was in the air. The cool breeze was refreshing. She walked from the house to the road which was about forty feet. Then strolled the same distance from the road to the creek For a moment she thought about and putting her feet in the cool waters of the creek. That idea came to an end when she remembered what the creek was like. It accumulated drainage from the mountains above the hollow. On its way down it picked up seepage from several abandoned mines. The water had such a high acid content that insects could not live near it.

There was a large boulder, somewhat like the shape of a bench, by the water's edge. She liked to sit there and let her mind wander. Carrying the baby over to the boulder, she sat down. The baby was awake but quiet, just like he must have known he should be. With the ripple of the water, with the over all quiet and coolness, Hilda's mind took flight.

It was fitting that this creek was called Willow Creek. It was named after Homer's grandfather. The Willow family had at one time owned most of the land in the hollow. That was before they knew that there was coal there and that it had much value.

The home that they lived in was originally his great grandfather's. The place was old and it had not aged gracefully.

The other children would be home in a few days and Hilda was looking forward to seeing them. Homer would be home in a few months. To Hilda, Homer was full of acid just like the creek. She was not looking forward to their private war starting all over again.

# *Chapter Three*

Hilda spent the last of the summer canning produce from the garden. This was a major project for her.

There was a flat yard that ran for about seventy-five feet behind the house. The garden was planted there. Beyond the garden there was a hill that started to go up very sharply.

She had planted the garden and religiously worked it all summer. For the past several weeks the garden had been paying off. Canning was tedious and it had to be done almost daily to keep up with the garden's production. Hilda took pride in the products she canned. She had learned well from her mother.

The house consisted of five rooms. It had three bedrooms, a kitchen with an eat-in area and a large living room. The house had a full basement. Aside from the coal bin, the walls of the basement were lined with plank shelving. It was on this shelving that the canned goods from the garden were stored.

Hilda had already canned peas, corn, tomatoes, tomato juice, pickles, relish, plums and filling for apple pies from trees in the yard. Only a few more things were left to be canned and soon she would be done. She knew she was getting close to the end of her canning as most of the shelving in the basement was filled.

One of the last things she made was chow-chow. It was made from the very last gathering from the garden. Things were picked just ahead of the first frost. The small immature items were chopped up and made into a semi-sweet relish.

It was Homer's favorite. Maybe that was why she didn't like to make it or maybe it was because it signaled the beginning of winter. Hilda preferred the summer. It let her get out of the house. She liked sitting by the creek and walking in the garden. Some people disliked garden work. Hilda on the other hand just loved it. She loved it because in a short period of time you could see the result of your efforts.

There was a natural spring at the base of the hill behind the house. It sat up about thirty feet higher than the house. The water was great and it ran year round. Before Homer was drafted, he boxed in the spring and ran a line to the house. Now they had running water inside the house.

Having running water in the house made it much easier for Hilda. With children ages three, two and three months she had plenty to keep her busy. She didn't need to be running to the spring for water all the time.

Her grandparents, who lived a few miles away, stopped by once every week or so to see how Hilda and their only grandchildren were doing. They usually brought something for the kids. They knew she was having a hard time while Homer was away in the army. She could always depend on them for help if it was needed.

Hilda had a fear that if someone saw the baby, they would be able to tell that it was too big to be a newborn. So far she had been able to come up with excuses not to have to show the baby. She was hoping to do this as long as she could.

The last time the grandparents were there the baby had been sleeping and she didn't want to disturb him. The next time they came she would have to show him. He had been with her now for almost two months.

Hilda heard some noise outside. It was grandfather. He had backed his truck to her basement window with a load of coal. He had brought a helper with him to shovel it into the basement. He was so understanding. He knew it would be getting cold soon and that she didn't have the money to buy coal.

After dumping the coal grandfather came inside to visit while the helper shoveled the coal through the basement window.

Hilda gave him a cup of coffee. Sitting at the kitchen table he simply asked, "When do I get to see the new baby?" Hilda braced herself. She knew she could not put it off any longer. She took him in the bedroom.

As they went into the bedroom the baby was asleep on its side. Just a side view of its head was showing from under the covers. Not enough of him was showing to cause any concern about his size.

Looking at the baby he said, "He sure is a beauty, just right for you but too nice for Homer. Hilda took in a deep breath and she felt relieved. Then she said, "Why would you say such a thing?" The hurt in her voice made him feel sorry for what he had said. He reached over and gave her a hug and said he was just kidding. He didn't mean to hurt her. Further, still in a kidding mood he said, "What I should have said was that he was too good look-ing to have come from Homer's side of the family. Seriously, he looks more like grandmother's side of the family."

Grandfather said that while his man was shoveling coal, Hilda should make a list of what she needed from town. He and grandmother were planning on stopping by on Sunday and he would bring the things with him. He knew how hard it was for Hilda to get anything from town even if she had the money. He smiled and said, "Let me get it this time." As he was leaving Hilda gave him a big hug and told him that he was truly a blessing in her life. She thought she saw a tear in his eye when he turned to walk away. As he had said many times, he did not like Homer and he did not like him marrying Hilda when she was fifteen. He would do anything for Hilda and the kids but as far as Homer was concerned, he could go to hell.

At one time he told Hilda that if she left Homer he would buy her a home and help her with the kids.

Grandfather had been the one who paid for the material for Homer to bring the water into the house. She doubted if she would have had water in the house if it had been left up to Homer.

A few weeks went by. Winter was trying to settle in. The hollow received its first light dusting of snow. The leaves were almost gone from the trees now.

There was only one house farther up the hollow, then Hilda's. The family's name was Plunk. Mister Plunk had been in the second world war. He had been shot up pretty bad. He could still get around but he spent most of his time in a wheel chair. There was just him and his wife, Barbara. Barbara was about thirty-five years old. She walked to town each day to work at the dry cleaners which was across the street from Dr. Rhodes office. Barbara was a nice lady and she helped Hilda whenever she could.

Dr. Rhodes had asked Barbara to drop off a note to Hilda on her way home. When she dropped off the note she said that the doctor said there might be an answer. If there was she would pick it up on her way to work in the morning. Hilda was to put it in the mail box.

The note said he would be coming out tomorrow at ten a.m. to visit Mister Plunk. While he was out there he wanted to stop by and see her and take a look at the baby. If there was anything she needed from town she was to leave the list for Barbara.

There were a few things she needed. Hilda had a charge account at the local grocery store. In the past the doctor had stopped and picked up things on his way out. This would save her a trip walking to town and she really appreciated it.

She doubted that the store would have given her credit if it had not been for grandfather. Since Homer had been away in the army grandfather had paid for almost all her groceries.

In the back of her mind Hilda was concerned about the doctor coming out. She wondered if something was on his mind other than the health of her baby.

Dr. Rhodes had been checking things out. He was trying to find out anything he could about the baby. He had gone over in his mind several times what Hilda had told him. Being aware of all the women from that area who had been pregnant at the time, he knew that none of them had a missing baby.

Hilda had described the basket and the surrounding fabric. That sounded like additional material had come from the basket.

Aside from checking the newspapers each day he listened to the news on the radio but nothing was ever mentioned.

If you were going to drop off a baby at someone's house, why not a good house? Why one that looked like this? Hilda's house was dilapidated and it was out of the way. Someone driving through town probably could not have even found the place much less drop off a baby there.

There was one incident that had occurred, a plane crash that same night. That was almost fifty miles away and everyone in that crash was burned beyond recognition. How could a baby end up fifty miles from the crash site? It looked like a second engine, running a little better for a short period of time, caused the plane to stay up long enough to fly out of the area where the baby was found. Maybe he could figure something out tomorrow when he visited Hilda and the baby.

The doctor drove by Hilda's to visit Mr. Plunk and then he stopped by on his way back. When he pulled up to the house Hilda went out to greet him. They each carried a box of groceries back to the house.

The doctor set about checking not only the baby but also, he took a look at the other two boys. Everybody checked out just fine.

After looking at the boys Hilda and the doctor sat at the kitchen table and had a cup of coffee. She thanked him again for bringing her the supplies from town. Dr. Rhodes said he wanted to talk to her about the baby. He mentioned how he had checked on everything he could think of. He even mentioned the plane crash. He asked Hilda to describe as best she could finding the basket again.

A thought crossed Hilda's mind. He had mentioned an airplane crash. All that fabric, all that string. My God, could it have been a parachute? She must have had an odd look on her face. The doctor said, "Are you alright, Hilda?"

"Yes, I'm fine," she said.

"Well, about the basket then."

She described the basket in great detail. She also described it being wrapped in a blanket in addition to the bedding that was in the basket. Hilda, however, left off this time what she described the last time as numerous sheets strings --- - and the doctor merely sat there with a puzzled look on his face.

Hilda's heart was pounding.

As if awakening from a daze he asked to see the blanket.

Hilda said that she had tore them apart looking for identification but found none. Then she discarded and burned everything.

"Dam," the doctor said. "You should not have done that." With that he took his last sip of coffee and left.

As the car pulled away Hilda sighed and sank down into one of her chairs.

After thinking it over for awhile she got up and got the kids ready for their nap. This done, she slipped out of the house. She walked to the sitting boulder by the creek. On a little high spot not far from the boulder she placed a statue of the virgin Mary. She had some praying to do. For the first time she felt that Jimmy was really going to be hers.

# *Chapter Four*

The worst of the winter had passed. It had been milder than most. It felt good just knowing that it was almost over. The children were doing fine. Jimmy had been seen by everyone and accepted as hers. No one even made a comment.

After grandfather made another delivery of coal it looked like they would have enough until spring.

Some of the earlier plants were just starting to leaf out. The days were getting longer. The nights were not quite as cold.

Jimmy fit in as part of the family. Once while Hilda was in town she called the newspaper office. It was about fifteen miles away. She asked about the plane wreck the doctor had mentioned. They said she was welcome to come in and look it up but they were too busy to handle it over the phone. Since she had no phone and no way of getting over to the newspaper office she let the matter drop.

Hilda started thinking about a birth certificate for Jimmy. She stopped by the doctor's office. She hoped there was some way he could help her. The doctor had been ahead of her and gave her the birth certificate. The certificate indicated that Jimmy had been born on August 25, 1953. He told Hilda it had already been registered. Hilda knew how lucky she was to have a friend like Dr. Rhodes.

Walking back to the house from the doctor's, Hilda realized that Homer would be coming home in a couple of weeks. In his last letter he indicated that he was going to be discharged from the army when he got back to the states. Homer expected to be back in April, the week after Easter.

Hilda thought this would give her enough time to get the house squared away. She surely wasn't looking forward to his coming home.

Homer was four years older than Hilda. After a few dates he had demanded sex. She had told him no but now felt she could have been a little stronger in telling him so. He forced himself on her and on that one occasion she got pregnant. She was in so much pain after the affair that she thought she would never have sex again.

After telling Homer about her condition, they decided to go out of state and get married. When they came home they set up housekeeping in the house where she was living now.

Not only had he not learned to be gentle with her while making love, he had even beaten her on several occasions. This was usually after he had been drinking. This was what she was looking forward to and she was very apprehensive.

When Homer got home he seemed to have changed somewhat. Hilda thought that maybe the army had made him grow up a little. She was pleased to learn that he had gotten a part time job while he was in Germany. With the extra income he had saved enough money to buy the kids some new clothes.

The pick-up truck he purchased when he came home was in pretty good shape. The few things that went wrong with it, Homer was well able to fix himself.

There was a new mine about to open up in the next valley over. Homer applied for a job there. He thought that his experience in the military service would help him secure it. He had been a motor vehicle repairman in the army. Basically, that was what he would be doing for the mine. He would be keeping the machines, both inside and outside the mine, in good working condition. The machine shop was situated outside of the mine so he would be spending very little time in the mine. This appealed to him because both his father and uncle had died with black lung disease. He didn't want to work inside the mine.

Homer got the job and things were looking up.

He was thankful that his military pay stayed in force until his new pay from the mine kicked in.

Homer seemed to be drinking less than Hilda had remembered. He had accepted Jimmy as his child without hesitation. He was even treating Hilda in a somewhat respectful manner. Their lifestyle seemed to settle into an acceptable routine. Hilda was pleased.

An uneventful year went by.

Hilda realized that she was expecting again. She gave Homer the news. He had mentioned several times that he didn't want any more children. That was fine but he didn't want to change any of his sex habits. He would not use protection and he forbid her to use anything. Hilda told him that it was just a matter of time before they would be in a family way again.

Upon hearing that she was expecting he angrily stormed out of the house.

He came back several hours later drunk and wanting to make love. He said, "Why the hell not make love? You can't get pregnant now, you already are."

He was very rough with her. The next day Homer was rough with her again. This was the first time he had been this way with her since getting home from the service. It was almost as if he wanted her to have a miscarriage. Unfortunately, this was the beginning of a change back to his old ways.

As the term of pregnancy progressed so did his drinking. He was stopping off almost every night on his way home from work. It was becoming unbearable.

When Homer's pick up truck drove up to the house, the children would scatter. Sometimes they would not come out until he had fallen into a drunken sleep.

Hilda had confided in Dr. Rhodes her concerns about Homer's behavior and the baby she was carrying. Homer had beaten her several times and once he kicked her in the stomach.

Dr. Rhodes, in addition to being the only doctor in town for several years, had almost become the town father.

The small town didn't have a police department. They were policed by the county. When a crime did occur, it would take thirty minutes to an hour before an officer would get there. Most of the problems between the people in the town were handled locally. Whenever domestic problems happened, usually, Dr. Rhodes was involved in some manner. Many times he would just sit down and talk to the people. They would see the error in their ways and change.

This is what Dr. Rhodes felt was needed with the Willows so he scheduled them to be his last appointment of the day. He told them the meeting was about Hilda's pregnancy and they both had to be there.

When they arrived the last patient and the nurse were leaving. They were alone in the office. Dr. Rhodes got right to the point. He told Homer that he was acting like an immature fool. If he didn't grow up and start treating his wife like a lady instead of beating her, he might just cause her to lose the baby. The doctor went on to tell

Homer that he had to get a handle on his drinking.

Homer, in so many words, told the doctor that it was none of his dam business. He got up without saying another word and left the office.

Hilda thanked the doctor for trying to help. She said she was afraid to go home but she thought it would be alright. As she left the office Hilda noticed that Homer's pickup truck was gone. He had left her so she had to walk home. She was concerned but when she made it to the house he was gone. She was relieved that he wasn't there. Mrs. Plunk had been baby sitting and she prepared to leave when when Hilda arrived. Mrs. Plunk made the comment that Homer had come home but he went right back out.

Hilda put the kids to bed.

She had cleaned up the house and was almost ready to go to bed when she heard Homer's truck drive up to the house. Shortly after that Homer came in. He was drunk and he let in to Hilda. He said, "To hell with your dam doctor. The good doctor's afraid that I will hurt the baby, is he? Well, take this." With his fist he hit her flush in the face. "Well," he said, "it shouldn't hurt the baby if I hit you in the face."

The force of the blow knocked her up against the wall and slowly she slid to the floor.

"Well," he said, "if I don't hit you in the stomach it should not hurt the baby, right?"

Hilda managed to get to her feet and he hit her again. This time he held her pinned against the wall and hit her three more times. She only remembered the second punch.

Hilda fell to the floor again. Blood was running from her nose and mouth. Her tongue was cut and bleeding as well. She laid there motionless.

Homer left her there and went to bed as if nothing had happened.

Some time during the night Hilda managed to get up off the floor and she made it to the couch. She spent the remainder of the night there.

The next morning Homer got up and went to work without checking on her or the kids.

Hilda pulled herself up from the couch and sat in a chair by the front window. Her head was pounding. She had to think hard to achieve any clarity. Her eyes were almost swollen shut. There was a feeling of sand in her mouth. It was dried blood.

She was watching for Mrs. Plunk. She finally came by. When she saw Hilda she came running. Hilda's face and shoulders were covered with blood. Her lips were swollen twice their normal size and there was a cut on the bridge of her nose that would need stitches.

Mrs. Plunk came into the house. She said, "My God, Hilda, what in the world happened?" She got some ice and made an ice pack for the swelling. She cleaned her up as best she could. The children were still sleeping.

Mrs. Plunk told Hilda to rest there and she would go and send the doctor out. She told Hilda that she could get off for the the rest of the day and she would be out to help with the kids.

When Mrs. Plunk told Dr. Rhodes about what had happened he dropped everything and headed out to Hilda's.

Upon his arrival he found Hilda in worse condition than he had expected. Fixing the facial damage was easy. Now he was worried about her unborn child.

The doctor felt in his heart that maybe his trying to fix things had actually made matters worse. He knew, however, there was only one person responsible for what had happened and it had to stop.

Dr. Rhodes had a lady on call who could come out and give him a hand with the children when Mrs. Plunk had to leave. He wanted Hilda to spend a few days at the clinic so he contacted her.

The next day in the clinic Hilda looked so much better. Hilda's facial injuries, although still quite a messy sight, did not present any real problems. The few stitches in her nose would leave a little scar but that wouldn't be so bad. The baby seemed no worse for the wear but the doctor was.

Every time he looked in on Hilda the doctor got madder. In the back of his mind a plan was taking shape. Some people would only learn in one way and this was one of those times. It was lesson time.

Almost everyone in that sparsely populated county owed at least one favor to the doctor. Some of them owed him many more.

The Kinch family a couple valleys over came to

mind. The first babies he delivered, almost twenty-five years ago, were the Kinch twins.

Mister Kinch came running into his office just as he was setting things up. He wasn't even open for business yet. Kinch ran in and took the doctor out to his car. It took both of them to get Mrs. Kinch into the clinic. Shortly thereafter she presented the world with  twin boys.

The Kinch family were not coal miners, they were farmers. They had a couple thousand acres of bottom land. They rarely came to town.

The boys had grown to manhood and most of the townspeople didn't know that they existed. They were schooled at home and had little contact with outsiders.

The only fighting they had done was between themselves and that was constant. That was good because they were both six feet five and two hundred seventy-five pounds.

The good doctor thought it was time to pay the Kinchs a visit.

The entrance to the valley where the Kinch farm was situated was via a dirt road that was carved along the edge of the mountain. The road sat up about two hundred feet above the valley floor. The crops were just getting started for the year. The panoramic view below was breath taking. You could see why the Kinchs didn't come to town very often. They had this beautiful world all to themselves.

As he drove up to the house the doctor noticed that two more homes had been built since he the last time he paid them a visit.

Seeing the him coming, Mr. Kinch came to greet him. There was a bond between the two men and it was apparent. Together, they went up on the shade of the porch. Mrs. Kinch brought them some lemonade and freshly made oatmeal cookies..

The doctor explained his problem to Mr. Kinch. He agreed it was lesson time for Homer. He said he could never understand how a man could hit a woman, much less the mother of his children. However, Mr. Kinch didn't want to see anyone permanently hurt. He insisted that the doctor be handy when it went down.

The Kinch's younger daughter went to get her brothers. When they arrived the doctor learned what the two new houses were for. Both of the boys had married since his last trip.

He told them about the man who constantly beat up on his wife. They were raised to know better and this alone pissed them off. When the doctor told them about him kicking her in the stomach and beating her up while she was pregnant they were ready to go.

A quick plan was made.

When Hilda was in the clinic Homer had to go straight home from work to look after the kids. He usually got home about three-thirty p.m.

The doctor asked Hilda if Homer owned a gun. She said she didn't think so.

In order to be safe, they were to let him get out of the truck. Then one would grab him and hold him while the other checked him and the truck for a gun.

The doctor would be waiting at the end of the dirt road. He planned to go out and check on Homer's condition when the twins left. He would see them as they drove by him on the way out.

The twins were to take Homer down to the creek. They would tell him why they were beating him. He had it coming because he was a punk and a wife beater. Then they would warn him if he ever beat her again they would be back. The next time it would cost him a couple of bones.

They were then to proceed to close his eyes and lay his nose flat on his face. A few kicks in the gut would also be in order.

The stage was set. Dr. Rhodes got Hilda out of the clinic and into his car. As they sat in his car by the clinic you could see the entrance to the dirt road that led to Hilda's house. They waited there until Homer's truck went by. Then they went down to the edge of the dirt road and waited.

Dr. Rhodes told Hilda that she had to be careful with Homer. He added however, that he thought she was going to see a big change in him. He considered telling her about what was going on in the hollow but after giving it some thought he decided against it. He had to tell her something. As an excuse he told her that he wanted to take some time with her to talk with her about the children.

She asked him what was on his mind?

He said he was wondering if Homer ever hurt the

children the way he had hurt her in the past? She said no, that she didn't think he had enough interest in the children to hurt them.

As Hilda talked the doctor was wondering what was going on up in the hollow.

Homer's truck pulled up in front of the house. As he got out of the truck, the two very large men, the twins, stepped from behind the wood pile. Homer shouted, "What the hell are you doing here?" One of them asked if he were Homer Willow? He said, "Yes."

With that answer one of the men grabbed him by the arms while they were down by his sides. Homer was only five feet ten inches tall and no more than one hundred forty pounds, almost half the size of the man holding him.

At first Homer didn't move as they checked him and the truck for a gun. Then suddenly he decided to kick the man who was holding him. This move was a mistake. His kick caught the man in the lower leg. This pissed him off. He grabbed Homer by his arms. With his big hands on each of his arms he picked him up like a sack of potatoes. Then he started to bang Homer's head on the hood of the truck.

The other brother came over and stopped the head banging. Then they walked Homer down to the creek. Homer had no idea what was going to happen. As they got him to the creek they turned him around and said, "Don't you know that only immature punks would beat up on a pregnant woman?"

Homer fit both of these descriptions. They asked him, "Do you know the only cure for such a problem?" A good ass kicking. With that the brother who was holding him hit him in the face. Then the other brother hit him three more times. Homer was almost out but they had more to say to him before they let that happen.

Homer was sitting with his back to a tree. One of the twins reached down and grabbed him by the neck. Turning Homer's face to him he said, "Look, wise ass, we aren't done with you yet. You never want to see us again. The next time you lay a hand on your wife and hurt her, we will be back again. If that happens you will wish you were dead. On that visit we will break your bones. Do you understand?"

Homer's eyes were rolling in  his head but he shook his head to indicate that he knew what they were saying.

They were turning to leave when Homer spit in their direction. One of the twins reached down and grabbed him by the hair with one hand and smacked him in the face with the other. When he was hit his head was against the tree. It made a funny sound and Homer was out cold. The other brother came over and kicked him in the lower stomach. He said that Homer wouldn't be bothering his wife in that area for some time to come.

The brothers walked back down the dirt road to where they had parked. They got in the truck and proceeded to drive out of the hollow. As they got close to town they saw the doctor, parked and waiting. He was out of his car and walking toward them. When he got to the truck he asked them if they were alright. They said, "Yes." He thanked them and they went on their way. When they pulled away he realized that he knew their names but not which one was which. The twins were so alike that he couldn't tell them apart.

The doctor walked back to his car and proceeded down the dirt road with Hilda. She asked him who those men were? He said he wasn't sure what their names were. As they approached the house nothing seemed out of order. When Hilda got out of the car she could hear faint moaning coming from the direction of the creek. She alerted the doctor and he got out of his car. Following the sounds to the creek, they found Homer by a tree. Barely conscious, he was a messy sight. His eyes were almost closed. Soon they would be swollen shut. He was covered with blood from his face down to the middle of his chest. Blood was running from his nose and mouth.

When the doctor got closer he could see that the job had been done. Maybe too well.

The doctor wanted to get Homer up to the house where he could work on him. He asked Homer to stand but he was having trouble getting up. With the help of the doctor, he managed to pull himself to a standing position but he was bent over almost double. That was because of the parting kick.

At the house the doctor cleaned Homer up. Aside from an ice pack and some pain pills there was little he could do for him. He determined that Homer's stomach was not ruptured. The pain medication was starting to take effect. They put him to bed. Dr. Rhodes was about ready to leave when Homer motioned him back.

Homer asked his wife to leave the room. When she was gone he turned to the doctor and said, "You had a hand in this, didn't you?" The doctor got close to the bed and said, "Homer, I am responsible for the health of all of the people around here." With that he turned and left.

# *Chapter Five*

Homer was out of work for almost two weeks. He had been very quiet around the house. There were several things he could have done while convalescing but he seemed to have little interest in them or in anything for that matter.

As time passed Homer showed little interest in Hilda. Part of his lack of interest in her could have been explained by her size. She was due to deliver in two months. Hilda thought Homer's reasons were deeper than that. Furthermore, his time spent with the children was more for the purpose of controlling them than teaching them anything. On occasion he had taken to spanking them. His spanking was a little too hard and Hilda was getting concerned. She didn't understand his change.

Finally, the time for the baby had arrived. Homer was at work when Hilda went into labor and she had to walk to the clinic. The birth was uneventful. The baby, a little girl, weighed in at eight pounds even. She had dark hair and blue eyes. When Homer saw her for the first time he commented on her eyes being blue. He said that the other children had dark eyes and he wondered where she had gotten her blue eyes. Hilda reminded him that Jimmy had blue eyes as well. Homer said, "That's right, I forgot."

Hilda thought to herself, you dumb ass. It made her feel a
little better knowing she had pulled one over on him.

With the new baby home Homer paid no attention
to Hilda. He was still getting after the boys on a regular
basis. Everything just seemed to settle into a groove and
time passed. It was rare when Hilda and Homer got
together, but that suited her just fine. She preferred it that
way. The kids had their usual share of childhood problems. Measles came and went. Then, the chicken pox and
other cold and nose drips. Time melted together. It didn't
seem possible but all the children were in school.

Kathy, their only daughter, was starting the first
grade. Jimmy was in the third, Bobby was in the fifth and
Billy was in the sixth. All were doing well and Jimmy was
at the top of his class. Hilda often wondered why he was
doing so well as he never seemed to study. With the kids
in school Hilda got an early start in the garden. She also
managed to have coffee with Mrs. Plunk, now and then.

Homer's drinking had started up again. He was
drinking heavily. This time he was taking it out more on
the kids. It was bothering Hilda so much that she often
cried herself to sleep at night. She told Dr. Rhodes about
Homer's behavior. He asked her if Homer had been hitting
her? She said she wished he would if that meant he would
leave the kids alone.

Homer had taken away almost all of Hilda's freedom. She had no transportation. Since their marriage he
had refused to teach her or to allow her to learn how to
drive. He kept a tight control on the money. She had no

idea what he made in the mine or where most of it went. She rarely had any money of her own. When she did it came from her grandfather. Mrs. Plunk couldn't understand why Hilda put up with Homer. Mrs. Plunk was her only contact with the outside world except for Dr. Rhodes and her grandfather. She felt more and more like the world was passing her by, and it was.

Homer was especially hard on Jimmy. Hilda tried but she couldn't understand why. She felt it might be because he was the brightest. Jimmy got a great deal of recognition from school. Since Homer never got such attention it must have pissed him off. For whatever reason he just wouldn't let up on the boy. Hilda could see that Jimmy was doing everything Homer asked him to do. He was made to do much more work around the house than the other boys. He did it without complaining but lately, he seemed to be withdrawing himself.

Jimmy had already grown bigger than Bobby. He was almost as big as Billy. It was obvious he was going to be the biggest of the three.

Jimmy was ten and starting the fifth grade. In school work he was at the top of his class. Jimmy's accomplishments did not impress Homer. He still treated him badly. It was as if he was hell bent on breaking him.

Behind the house, where the hill went up, there was a seam of coal. The seam started about waist high and went up about two and one half feet. This type of outcropping was common in the area. Homer told Jimmy that they needed ten tons of coal for the winter. He told him he could spend his summer digging that coal and bringing it to the house in a wheel-barrow. Like the other tasks that he had been assigned, Jimmy set out to do what he was told.

Jimmy was too small to bring a full wheelbarrow load of coal at a time. His hands had hardened up since he first had blisters from the work. It broke Hilda's heart to watch him working so hard when the other boys were playing. She asked them to help him but they said if they did Homer said he would beat them. Watching Jimmy work burned out the last bit of feeling Hilda had for Homer. All that remained was hate. She asked for God's forgiveness when she actually wished that Homer was dead.

Jimmy worked a full day, weather permitting. He could move to the house about one half a ton of coal a day. Then it still had to be shoveled into the basement. He would spend a few days bringing the coal to the house. When the pile got big enough he would spend most of the day shoveling it into the basement.

One day in August, Homer came home from work drunk. He saw Jimmy bringing a wheelbarrow of coal to the house. He looked at the load and wanted to know why it wasn't full. Jimmy told him it was all he could carry. Homer angrily slapped him across the face and went into the house and down to the basement. In the basement sat about eight tons of coal. He went back outside and saw a pile, about another half ton, by the basement window. Jimmy had dumped another load and was going for a drink of water. Homer grabbed him by the hair and said, "Boy, you are coming with me. You should have had the coal in the house already and you are just goofing off." In fact, poor Jimmy was breaking his back to do what his father had told him. Hilda saw it all and she was concerned.

Homer headed to the creek with Jimmy. As he passed the wood pile he picked up a piece of rope. Hilda watched from the house. Seeing Homer with the rope, she ran out and tried to stop him. He hollered at her to stay back or she would get some of the same. He tied Jimmy's hand to the overhead branch of a tree. Then he pulled Jimmy's shirt over his head. He reached and undid his own belt. In his drunken rage he said, "This will teach you to do what you are told."

Homer began hitting Jimmy over his bare back. The first five slaps with the belt welted up his back. Then Homer paused momentarily. Maybe not even knowing it he turned the belt around. Now his big belt buckle was on the end of the belt that was striking Jimmy. As he was being hit Jimmy didn't cry. He just moaned as the belt buckle cut into his back. After seeing the belt bite into his back Hilda couldn't stand it anymore. She rushed over and gathering all of her strength, she shoved Homer aside. Homer did not seem to care any longer. He put his belt back on and got into his truck and left..

Hilda cut Jimmy down from the tree. He was still moaning. All he said was, "Mom, what did I do wrong?"

"Nothing son, nothing," she answered. She knew

he wasn't hers but right then she loved him more than anything else on earth. Hilda helped Jimmy to the house.

Billy ran to summon the doctor. He rode back to the house with the doctor in his car. Jimmy was dirty all over from working with the coal. As the doctor looked at Jimmy, Hilda saw a tear in the doctor's eye. He talked softly to him as he treated him gently. After he finished with him he told Hilda that he wanted to take Jimmy to the clinic. He wanted to keep an eye on him in case of infection. Appreciative, Hilda thanked him for helping them.

After being in the clinic for a few days the burning on Jimmy's back stopped. The doctor checked in on him several times a day. Jimmy liked him. He felt that Dr. Rhodes was the only person who really understood how he was feeling. The doctor decided to keep him there for a few more days until the stitches came out. He was actually enjoying Jimmy's presence and wasn't looking forward to his leaving.

After Jimmy had gone home Dr. Rhodes asked Hilda to come in and see him. He wanted to find out what had happened to set Homer off against Jimmy. She told him about the event that led up to the beating. He could not believe it. He asked how she and Homer were getting along and he wasn't surprised when she told him. She said she would do anything to get rid of Homer but she had no way of taking care of the children without him. She was also pretty sure that he had another woman. The doctor said that since she already knew he would tell her that he had heard that Homer did, in fact, have a girlfriend.

The doctor told her to go home but not to let Homer know that she knew about his girlfriend. He had a few calls to make and he might be able to help her out.

Hilda was the doctor's last visitor for the day. For him this day couldn't end fast enough. The good doctor had a close feelings for Jimmy. Maybe it was the way he arrived, or just the nice young man that he was. He felt that he had some planning to do. It would probably take another trip to the Kinchs for their help in giving that ass hole another lesson.

The next morning the doctor left early for his office. He got there and wrote down his plans for the day. When his nurse came in he told her that they would only be open for half a day. She was instructed to call the afternoon patients and re-schedule them for tomorrow.

Finished with his last patient, the doctor was out the door with note pad in his hand. As he left the office he headed his car down the dirt road to Hilda's. She was out in the yard, hanging clothes, when he arrived. They went into the house and had coffee at the kitchen table. They talked for awhile about Homer and the fact that she had rather be without him. Dr. Rhodes got right to the point.

"Hilda, I know that you would leave him in a minute if you thought you could handle the kids without him. You know I will try to help you in any way that I can. There are some things that I have to do to make everything come out the way you would like. I want you to tell Homer tomorrow that you want a divorce. Be sure not to let on to him that anything is up until then. Will you do that?"

"Hell, yes I will, but why tomorrow?"

"I don't want to discuss it now but like I said, there are a few things I have to do. It is agreed then. Tomorrow when Homer comes home from work you will ask him for divorce and tell him to leave the house."

As the doctor was leaving he assured her that everything would be alright.

Hilda didn't know what to say. She thanked the doctor. As he left she couldn't tell if she was happy or sad. She just hoped that whatever he did worked out and that she would be free of Homer.

Driving down the dirt road the doctor looked at his notes. The next stop would be the Kinch farm. He wondered if he was doing the right thing. He wasn't sure but he knew that if he did nothing he would not be able to live with himself. Unfortunately, there was no rule book for him to follow in a case like this. Maybe someone should write one, it would probably sell. The title would be, "How To Cure An Abusive Asshole." Homer could be the first case of study.

Coming around the bend in the road that led to the Kinch farm, as usual, you almost had to catch your breath when you first saw that great view. Only Mrs. Kinch was at the house when he drove up. She came out and greeted him. Shortly thereafter, the others came from the other houses.

Since the last time he had come calling for help,

both of the Kinch twins had started families. They each had three children. It didn't seem that long ago.

While he was there he took a look at the children. They set up a mini-office in the kitchen and the children were brought in one at a time. They were all in good health. Knowing that he was coming out, the doctor had reviewed their shot records back at the clinic. He had come prepared to give them shots up to date. The children weren't too happy but the family appreciated it.

With this behind them the four men sat at the table to hear the real reason the doctor had come to visit. He gave them the details. They were as sick about the matter as he was. "What in the hell makes this man this way?" said Mr. Kinch. "There is no doubt in my mind that if it were one of my boys doing something like that I would take a piece of two by four to him. How can we help you doctor? Then they discussed the matter in great detail. Another lesson plan was worked out for the following day. The doctor thanked them and left.

Looking down at his note pad again, he set his direction to the mine where Homer worked. The mine was actually about half way back to town. Dr. Rhodes knew Mr. Kozel, the foreman of the mine. He had just helped him over a rough time with his mother.

Driving up to the mining office, he went in where he was greeted by the receptionist. She said that Mr. Kozel was expecting him and she showed him into his private office. Mr. Kozel seemed a little excited when the doctor entered. Then he realized that his nurse had made the appointment and Mr. Kozel must have thought there was something wrong with his mother. Closing the door behind him, he put Mr. Kozel at ease.

He said he had come there for help on another problem. Mr. Kozel said he would be glad to help and asked what the problem was? The doctor went over the story again. Mr. Kozel sat there for a few moments with a pensive look on his face. Then he said, "I'll be dammed, you know, doctor, it's hard to believe we are talking about the same person. As a matter of fact, the man who is head of the department where Homer works is retiring. He had recommended Homer as his replacement. Homer has done good work for us. I guess he can kiss that promotion good-bye."

"No," the doctor said, "that makes it even better. If he has done good by you he has earned what you have planned for him. He will have more money for his child support payments. That way he will have to pay more for the problem he has caused." Mr. Kozel agreed.

The doctor said he had come there to find out how much money Homer made. That way when his wife got her divorce she ask for the proper amount of child support. She could get a court order and have it taken right out of his pay.

Mr. Kozel said it would be a pleasure to see that bastard have to pay. He would be glad to assist by deducting it. He gave the doctor the amount of his present pay and the amount he would be making after his promotion. He expected the promotion to take place in a week or ten days. The last thing he said was, "If the doctor had asked to pick a man who worked for him that was a wife and child beater, Homer would have been way down on his list."

The doctor thanked him, said goodbye, and headed for his next appointment. As he was driving he tried to get his thoughts together for his next meeting. He had no idea how it would go. He had no favors coming from Mr. Welch, who happened to be the only lawyer in town. He had been there for a only few years. The doctor know little about him and his family but of what he did know, none of it was bad.

There were no other clients in Mr. Welch's office when the doctor arrived. He started to explain what the problem was. Before he could finish Mr. Welch stopped him. He said, "First, I am glad you came to see me about this problem. Second, a few days ago I had a visit from Homer. He wanted to discuss getting a divorce. He hadn't made his mind up when he left and he didn't retain me as his lawyer. It was just a discussion and a short one at that. I don't believe he knows what he wants to do yet. He talked about child support. He wanted to know if he got a divorce and had to pay support would it go up later if he got a pay raise?"

"That bastard," the doctor said. He told Welch about Homer's pending promotion at the mine. Welch had been sitting on the fence. This pushed him off.

Mr. Welch and Dr. Rhodes spent the next hour laying a plan to get the most they could for Hilda and the kids from Homer. Knowing that he was such an ass added a little zest to their planning.

The doctor told him that Hilda would be in to see him tomorrow afternoon. He told him everything except about the up coming Kinch lesson. When the doctor left he felt that he had found another friend. They had agreed to pay for their services by swapping time. So far he owed the good lawyer one hour for services rendered. A hell of a deal.

The doctor got home late for supper. The food was prepared and on the back of the stove. His house lady was his next door neighbor. She only worked for him about an hour a day doing odds and ends around the house. For his supper she usually brought over a portion of what she was fixed for her own family. Fortunately, she was a good cook and the arrangement worked out well, especially on a day like today. The doctor was tired but he felt good inside. Things had gone well and he was looking forward to tomorrow.

The next day the doctor got to his office early. He wanted to be organized when people started coming through the door. Today, he was working a little faster than normal. He wanted to be finished by half past three. With a short lunch he made it.

As planned he was on watch when Homer turned the corner and headed out the dirt road. He went back on station where the twins would pass him on their way out.

Homer pulled up and got out of his truck. He had a habit of walking around the side of the house and entering through the kitchen door. Homer went around the side of the house and was almost to the kitchen door when he noticed one of the twins coming toward him. He turned around to head back to the truck but the second twin was right behind him. Homer knew what was coming. He punched his fist at the first twin but he just caught it and put his arm behind his back. They were taking him back toward the creek again.

Homer felt helpless and said, "Oh shit," as he was pushed forward. As they went past the wood pile there was some rope there just as if someone had planned it. They picked up the rope and continued on. A little further toward the creek they noticed a large overhanging tree branch. It had a small piece of white rag tied to it as if someone was trying to tell them something. Homer didn't pick up these little markers.

They tied Homer's hands over his head to the tree. They took his shirt off just like he had done to Jimmy. They asked him how a small boy might feel if someone did this to him. He told them to go to hell. They said, "Homer, we told you that you wouldn't like it if we came back. A long black whip was brought out and they proceeded. Homer cried like a baby but they didn't stop until his back as a bloody mess. He was barely alert when they stopped.

One of the twins leaned over and grabbed him by the hair, turning his face toward him and said, "The next time you take advantage of anyone, it will be your last. So you will remember this and what an ass hole you are every time you look in the mirror, I'll leave you with this." He pulled a small wrench from his pocket and knocked out his two front teeth. Then they got back in their truck and waved to the doctor on their way out.

The doctor drove out to the house. He knew what to expect when he got there. Still, the condition of Homer's back was worse than he figured it would be. Hilda helped him cut Homer down. With both helping they managed to get him to the house. After he was cleaned up he looked better. He only needed a few stitches in his back. His mouth had stopped bleeding and he was able to drink some water.

When she was sure he could hear and understand what she was saying, Hilda told Homer that she wanted a divorce. At first he said nothing. Then he said, "If that's what you want it's just fine with me." She said she wanted him out of the house right then. He said, "You go to hell. If you want a divorce you get the hell out of the house."

The doctor said that with the kids, she would need the house much more than he did. In addition he said that there were plenty of people around who might think that he was taking advantage of his wife and children if he stayed.

"Didn't them big boys tell you that you had better not take advantage of anyone or they would be back?"

Homer said, "Screw you Doc, I always knew you were involved with those bastards."

"If you feel that way, then you could be sure they would hear about you kicking your family out of the house."

Homer became silent. He didn't say another word. He got up, packed a bunch of clothes and took them out to his truck. On his last trip, he asked Hilda if she would put the rest of his clothes on the porch. He would come by tomorrow to pick them up.

As the pickup truck pulled away from the house the doctor gave Hilda a hug. She sighed and said, "Thank God that's over with." Dr. Rhodes thought to himself that he wished to hell it really was.

# *Chapter Six*

After Homer left Hilda felt a sigh of relief. When she had time to think about it she wondered if she was doing the right thing. The doctor had said he would help her. She hoped she could depend on him. Hilda wondered just how much help could be really done with a high school drop out with four kids.

Hilda was on her way to meet the lawyer. She was wondering what she was going to say. She had all of ten dollars in her purse. How could she begin to pay him? Regardless, she knew she had to see him and she hoped he would be understanding of her predicament..

Mr. Welch put her at ease as soon as she walked in. He seemed to already know what she wanted. She asked him how he knew? He told her he had had a visit from the doctor. He was sorry for what she was going through with Homer. He felt there would be little trouble in getting her the assistance that she needed in the divorce.

She asked him what he thought that was? He went into detail. He thought that she should get the use of the house, child support for the children and then some money for her. She just asked one more question. Would it be enough to take care of the kids? He said they might be able to get by but he felt that she probably would have to get some kind of job.

From there they went over dates and times. They discussed where Homer worked, the names and ages of the children, the date of their marriage, and so forth. She asked how long it would take to get the divorce? He said that would depend. If Homer contested any demands they make it could take awhile.

"Demands, like what?" she asked.

"Well, he could claim that you haven't been a good mother and he could want the children."

"He won't do that. I don't think he ever wanted the children in the first place."

"He might say you cheated on him."

"He was my one and only man."

"Well, I think you see what I mean."

Mr. Welch looked at Hilda closely for the first time. He asked her how old she was? She answered that she was twenty-nine. She had been with Homer for almost fifteen years. He had a hard time believing her age but he knew it was true. She still had a good figure but her hair style detracted from her appearance. She took care of it herself and it left a little something to be desired. Her face had never seen makeup. Added to that, her shoes and the old dress she was wearing made her look at least forty years old.

He told Hilda that he planned to file the necessary divorce papers that afternoon. She could expect to hear from him in a couple of days. They would try to set up a hearing as soon as possible.

With the discussion over she got up and headed toward the door. She stopped for a moment and turned to ask him how much this was going to cost? He said a friend of hers had taken care of it. She asked who it was? He said if the individual wanted her to know they would tell her. She turned to go again and this time he said, "I have one last question. Has your husband been cheating on you?"

She answered, "yes," and continued out the door.

Walking home she wondered who it might be that was helping her. There were only two people that came to mind. The doctor and her grandfather. As she walked by the grocery store she stopped for a few items. They would no longer give her credit. Fortunately, she had enough money to pay for the items she had selected. On her way home she figured that Homer must have stopped by the store and told them that he would no longer be paying her bills. Now she had no doubt. He cared nothing for the children. What she was doing was for the best.

When she arrived home her grandfather was sitting outside in his car. She invited him into the house. For the first time she noticed the hard time he was having getting out of the car. His age had finally caught up with him. Two years ago grandmother had died in an old folks home. She was a few years older than he was. At that time he could still do a good days work. She was now wondering how long she would have him.

He had heard the news that she was getting a divorce. He was glad she was finally leaving Homer. He had not been one of his favorite people. Grandfather said he never minded getting old until now. If he were thirty years younger he would enjoy kicking Homer's ass.

He wanted to know if everything was alright. She assured him that it was. She also told him about the visit from the twins. He said he had heard about that.

"Well then," Hilda said, "you seem to know all there is to know about me. Do you know that my grocery account has been shut off?"

"No," he said that he had not heard about that but he would fix it when he went back to town.

He asked her what her plans were? For the first time she realized that she had none.

"Are you going to stay here? Because if you are I am going to get you a phone for this God forsaken place. At least with a phone you will be able to give me a call if you have some trouble. Hilda said she had no other place to go.

When he got up to leave he came over and gave her a kiss on the cheek. He handed her a hundred dollars and said he wished it could be more. He mentioned that it had taken much more to take care of grandmother at the home than he had planned on. He said he would always be there for her. He laughed and said all she had to do was call. That was when she got a phone. His parting words to her were that he had left his home to her in case something happened to him.

Hilda watched him get into the car and she didn't like what she saw. She hoped she wouldn't be moving into his home for some time.

Homer contested the divorce when he found out what the demands were. The hearing was put off for a few weeks so they could meet and hopefully come up with some kind of agreement. Homer had found an attorney from the other side of the county to represent him. The meeting was set.

Hilda and Homer attended the meeting with their two lawyers. They sat across the table from each other.

The doctor and Mr. Welch had done their homework. After Homer insisted that she receive practically nothing, Mr. Welch opened up his note pad and started to read some of his notes. He said, "Homer, you stop me in case I say something that isn't true." He mentioned Homer's beating and kicking Hilda when she was expecting a baby. He reminded him of his requiring Jimmy do a man's work at the age of ten and of his brutally beating him for not completing a job within his unreasonable time frame. The lawyer had several other choice stories to tell. Finally he brought up the subject of Homer's girlfriend.

With that Homer stood up and said, "Now that's all bull shit."

Then Mr. Welch mentioned the name of the girl and the fact that she was expecting. Homer sat down and put his head down on the table. Hilda just sat there with a blank stare as if she was out to lunch. She suddenly realized that she didn't have a single feeling for the man sitting across from her. Mr. Welch kept on reading from his list. Then he listed the names of eight people who had agreed to come forward and testify on Hilda's behalf.

Homer's lawyer sat there mute and shook his head. Finally he said, "Boy, that don't sound one dam bit like the story you told me." He suggested that they go over the demands one at a time and he advised Homer to agree to them. He mentioned that some of the items that had been brought up were against the law. If this went to a full scale hearing, Homer might be charged with a crime and have to do time. That got Homer's attention.

They went down the list and Homer agreed to all of it. Hilda got the use of the house until the youngest child was eighteen. Homer had to pay a small amount of alimony. Then came the matter of child support. The amount asked for was larger than his lawyer thought was fair. He asked Mr. Welch what he based his numbers on? Homer hadn't told him about the promotion. His lawyer's face said it all as he looked at Homer. There was one last item. Mr. Welch had papers drawn up to allow the money to be taken right out of Homer's pay. Homer signed them and they were witnessed. It was over. The lawyers would take care of the paperwork. Hilda was free for the first time in her adult life.

As she was leaving the office Mr. Welch told her that Dr. Rhodes wanted her to stop by his clinic on her way home. Hilda wondered what he wanted but she was soon to find out.

There were two things he wanted to discuss with her. First, he wanted to know what happened at the lawyer's office. Second, he wanted her to consider working in his office three days a week. The work was mainly keeping the place neat and clean. She thought about the doctor's offer for several minutes. Then she agreed to take the job. She wouldn't start for a week or so though. She needed time for her new status to sink in.

Hilda left the office and started home. Walking down that dirt road was different this time. She couldn't put her finger on it but things she had never noticed before, that must have been there for years, looked just beautiful. The road seemed softer under her feet. Somehow she felt taller. Maybe it was the heavy weight she had just lifted from her shoulders. Tomorrow was looking better already.

# *Chapter Seven*

After Hilda got home she poured herself a cup of coffee and sat down. She was going over everything that had happened, trying to make sense out of it. Then she tried looking at the future. She didn't like everything that she saw, but not having to worry about Homer coming home from work anymore made her feel that it had all been worth the effort.

Her life would change forever now and she was trying to get a handle on it.

The days went by. She noticed grandfather coming out more often than he had before. He was spending more time with the boys and she liked that. He even began helping them with their homework. It was then that Hilda found out that he had been to college for two years. She hadn't even thought about college for the boys. That seemed more like a dream.

It had snowed more than usual that year, particularly on the mountains above the hollow. Several days ago the rain had started, slow at first but steady. The house in the hollow sat up several feet above the creek. The creek was starting to come up. Hilda was getting a little worried. She walked out of the house toward the creek. Her favorite stone bench was under water. She could see quite a ways down the dirt road toward Franklin. Parts of the road were now under water. She got Jimmy and they started to move things from the front yard to the rear of the house which was higher.

About two hours alter she took another look at the creek. It had come up two or three feet in that time. It was now more than half way to the house. She looked down the dirt road again and knew that they could not make it out. She wondered how the people in town were doing. She didn't think the water would harm the house but she was concerned that it might flood out the basement. Just two years ago Jimmy and Bobby had resealed the foundation because of a rat problem and because some water was getting in from the run off from the roof.

Hilda went outside one more time for a look before darkness set in.. The creek was now fifteen feet from the house. She could see that large trees and boulders were being washed down the hollow.

The combination of snow melting and heavy rains had turned the creek into a monster. The phone was dead. There was nothing anyone could have done to help anyway. The power was out and Hilda was up all night with a flashlight. She watched as the creek inched its way up to the house. About one a.m. the rain stopped. At first light the creek was at the first step of the porch coming into the house. About two hours later it had quit coming up. Just before lunch the creek started going down.

Hilda had forgotten about the basement. She went over to the basement door and opened it slowly, expecting the worst. She turned on the flashlight. The basement was as dry as a bone.

The following day some men from town came out with a four drive vehicle. They told them that the flood had taken the lives of several people from Franklin. They said it would be a few more days before a car could go down the dirt road. They asked Hilda if they needed anything. If she did, they would make another trip out for her.

The small black and white television that they had had for years, finally died. Grandfather took it to town to see if it could be fixed. It was pronounced dead upon arrival. He purchased them a new twenty-one inch color set and brought it out to the house.

When the kids got home from from school he sat them down and made some rules. First, there would be no watching television after nine p.m. on school nights. Secondly, all homework had to be done before you could watch it. Third, anyone with less than a B average would have to do extra studies before they could watch it. All the kids were getting a B or better. He just wanted to keep it that way. He brought a chart with him and hung it on the basement door. The chart was a calender that you could sign off when your work was done. For the next several days he came out to help with the homework, then he got back to his usual two or three times a week. The children played by the rules and their school work went up a notch.

A couple of months went by. Hilda was working three days a week at the clinic and she liked it. One day grandfather came to visit her while she was working. He apparently had been talking to the nurse who worked there. The nurse, grandfather and Hilda went to lunch together. At lunch grandfather told Hilda that she needed to take better care of her personal appearance. He reached into his pocket and pulled out five hundred dollars. He said, "Hilda, this is for you on the condition that you spend it all on yourself.

Hilda couldn't believe it. She and the nurse had the afternoon off so they made an appointment to have Hilda's hair done after lunch. Then they went shopping to buy her some cosmetics and new clothes. The nurse helped Hilda select the clothing and apply the cosmetics.

Hilda was like a young girl. Some time later she was to find out that grandfather had sold an antique piece of furniture that had been in the family several generations in order to get the five hundred dollars.

Before the make over Hilda looked older than her age. Now with her new appearance she looked younger than her age. She not only looked better but she was starting to catch the eyes of some of the men in town.

Hilda was about five feet seven inches tall. She had always been trim. With all the work she had to do at the house with the kids and the garden she never put on the pounds. Her figure had always been outstanding but you couldn't tell it with the type of clothes she wore. Her eyes were a deep, piercing blue. Her hair was dishwater blond with no particular style. Hilda for the the first time in her life was was getting a complete make over.

The results were outstanding. Her hair was cut and

lightened a shade or two. The lighter blond hair made her blue eyes stand out all the more. The new clothes showed her figure off. She was a knockout! Suddenly, she seemed to walk with self-assurance. A new lady had come to town.

Mr. Welch, the lawyer, walked past her twice in the grocery store without even recognizing her. If she had not spoken he never would have known it was Hilda. When he realized who she was he couldn't believe his eyes and told her so. She blushed and turned away. Hilda was almost thirty years old and that was the first time that a man had complimented her.

Everyone in the grocery store had been talking about the big cold wave that was headed their way. So far this winter it had been milder than normal. It had only snowed a couple of times and luckily the temperature had not fallen below zero.

As Hilda arrived home the weather was steadily changing. It had been very cold walking on the road from town. She was glad she had plenty of coal in the basement. When they went to bed that night it was hard to keep the inside of the house warm. Everyone took an extra blanket for his bed.

About two in the morning Hilda woke up. It was about forty degrees in the house. The house was poorly insulated and the old furnace wasn't doing a very good job. To make matters worse she found that the rear door had been left ajar.

Jimmy was already down in the basement getting

the old furnace going as well as he could. He suggested that they cut off the heat to all the rooms except Hilda's room and the kitchen. Kathy could move in with her and the boys could move into the kitchen. With that adjustment they were able to keep the temperature at sixty-five degrees.

That morning, on the radio, they learned that it was the coldest day in the history of the area. About noon they put on the heaviest clothing they had and went outside. There had been a three inch snowfall. Everything was frozen hard. They walked down to the creek and it was frozen over. That was the first time Hilda could remember it happening. The creek was solid ice and one could walk across it. The weather stayed that way for several days before it got back to normal.

Things started to settle into a groove once again and some time passed. The children had really grown. Billy was fifteen and in the tenth grade. Bobby was fourteen and in the ninth grade. Jimmy was twelve and in the seventh grade. Kathy was ten and in the fifth grade.

All of the children were doing well in school. Jimmy, as in the past, was well ahead of his grade. The school had begun to let him have books from the grades ahead of him. In his class they used him as a teacher's aid. He usually assisted three or four of the slower kids.

Jimmy was ahead in other ways as well. He was five feet ten and going up. He was also about one hundred fifty pounds. He was bigger than his older brothers. For someone his size he was well proportioned. His body was filling out very nicely.

Hilda was concerned about Jimmy because he seemed to be distant, at times. At other times he was nowhere to be found. She needed to talk to him. She asked Jimmy to come down to the sitting rock at the creek one day. There she expressed her concerns to him. She asked him where he went at times when they couldn't find him.

He said he liked the place by the creek where she often came. She said I like it, too. He said that he had found a place that he liked as well and it was his special place like this was hers. She asked where it was? He was reluctant to tell her, at first, but she insisted.

"Well," he said, "I can tell you about it but if you want to see it I will have to show you."

"Tell me about it first."

Jimmy said that one day last summer while he was picking blackberries for her to make jam, he found it. The briars were very thick. As he pushed through them to get to the berries he noticed that they were covering what looked like the entrance to an old abandoned coal mine. He cut through the briars enough to get in. The opening was about five feet high and five feet wide. He walked in as far as he could go with what light was coming from the entrance. It was a hot day so he stayed inside the cool entrance for a while.

The next day he came back with a light and went in to the end. It was a tunnel not a mine. It went from their hollow to the other side of the hill. It was only about three or four hundred feet long. The entrance on this side was just above the level of the creek. When it came out on the other side it was about two hundred feet above the valley floor.

The view from the other side was spectacular. Jimmy had taken an old bench over there and he liked to sit there and study or just relax and read a book. There was usually a soft cool breeze coming from the tunnel that was refreshing. Hilda insisted that he show her.

The next day with both of them carrying a light they entered the tunnel. She could see why no one had noticed it before. Even the opening that Jimmy had cut into the entrance did not expose it to view. Once inside the tunnel, you had to bend over to avoid hitting your head on the ceiling.

On the way over Hilda noticed some old miners lamps. They were like some of the ones she had seen when she was a kid. She pointed them out to Jimmy and said they should pick them up on their way back.

As they came out on the other side she could see why Jimmy liked coming there. The view was fantastic! She stood there for a minute just drinking it all in. On the valley floor were several small farms. You could see all around for miles. So this was Jimmy's quiet place! She loved it as well and saw no reason to change anything. For awhile it was like looking at a Norman Rockwell painting.

Hilda asked Jimmy to string a wire through the tunnel with a can or something on the end of it. If she ever needed to get hold of him she could pull the wire and he could answer. Jimmy said that he would. As they were getting back to the house she said, "Lets just keep this as our little secret."

A few days later Hilda cleaned up the lamps she found in the tunnel and took them to work. She put them on a desk in the reception area. Mr. Kozel, from the mine where Homer worked, happened to come in that day. While he was waiting for his appointment he inspected the lamps. When he was leaving he asked who they belonged to and he was told that they were Hilda's. He asked her where she had gotten them? She didn't want to tell him about the tunnel so she said that one of her boys had found them in an old mine shaft. To her surprise he asked if he could take one and check it out. He promised to give it back in a couple of days. As he was leaving he suggested that Hilda put the other lamp up, that it might be of some value. After he left she put it in the closet with her cleaning supplies.

One afternoon grandfather drove up to the house. There was a second man following him in a car. He came up to the door and asked Hilda to come outside. He showed her the second car and told her that he had bought her a car.

She said, "That's fine but I don't know how to drive."

He answered not to worry that part of the terms of purchase had been driving lessons from Joe, the man who had driven the car out. Then, he introduced her to Joe Evens. Joe handed her a driving manual and asked her when it would be convenient for him to come back and start her lessons. They decided on Friday afternoons at four.

While Joe was showing the car to the boys Hilda thanked her grandfather. He said he was sorry it had taken so long but he had he wanted to get the right car. He said the guy at the local Ford dealership was an old friend of his and he had been watching out for a good deal. The car was four years old but it had only eight thousand miles on it. The lady who had it new only drove it about a year. She had an accident at home and she had to be put in a care facility. The car just sat there until she passed away. At least, now it would be put to some good use. What grandfather didn't tell her was that the car cost him the last of his antique furniture.

During the next two days Hilda read the driving manual front to back twice. By the time Friday came around she had read it a third time. She also found the operators manual in the glove compartment of the car and read that. Somehow Joe had obtained a copy of the test they gave for the driving license. After asking her a few questions he gave her the test. She got all of the answers right except the one on insurance. She hadn't even thought about insurance. The driving lesson went alright. Joe said she had done very well.

Hilda started thinking about insurance. She would only be driving from her house to town. Then she thought about Billy. In a year or so he would be wanting to get his license. She couldn't take a chance. She would have to get insurance.

Hilda talked to the doctor getting car insurance. He told her the name of his agent and even made the call for her. He talked to the agent explaining the minimum coverage that she would need. Then Hilda gave the agent the information about the car. The agent asked her about her driving record. She said that she had never had an accident nor been given a ticket. The doctor was still listening to the conversation and with her answers a smile came to his face. The agent said he would call back later with a price for her. She thanked him and hung up the phone. She and the doctor had a good laugh. Hilda didn't laugh. however, when he called back with the price. The insurance was going to cost ninety dollars. Just then, that was ninety dollars she did not have.

For the last couple years Billy had had a paper route. He delivered papers in the morning and evening. It wasn't so hard on him. In the morning they would leave his papers at the end of the dirt road and he would deliver them on his way to school. In the afternoon they would drop his papers off at his first stop and he would deliver them on the way home. He had made a deal with Hilda that he would give her half the money he made. He would use the other half for buying his school clothes and for pocket change.

The grocery store in town was looking for a box boy. Hilda had an idea. She asked Billy if he had rather have that job as it paid more money. He said, "Yes." She talked to Bobby about the paper route and he agreed to take it. They both would be giving half their pay to their mother. Now Hilda could afford to buy insurance on the payment plan.

After a few more lessons Hilda managed to get her driver's license. Very soon she realized how much help having the car was and she didn't know how she ever did without it.

Mr. Kozel stopped by the clinic to see her one day. He brought the lamp he had borrowed back with him.He said he checked them out and as he thought they had some value. His company had been in the mining business for years and they had a collection of old mining items in their home office. He offered her three hundred dollars for each of the lamps. In need of money, of course she agreed to sell them. She tried to recall where she had put the other lamp. Then she remembered she had put it in the closet. She said she would be right back. She went to the closet but couldn't find it. Searching frantically, finally she noticed it sticking out under a pile of dirty towels. She gave the second lamp to Mr. Kozel and he sat down and wrote her a check for six hundred dollars.

Hilda went to the bank and deposited the money right after work. This was the largest balance she had ever had in her account. On the way home she thought about what she could do with the money. She decided to keep it as a rainy day fund.

Joe, the man who gave her the driving lessons, asked Hilda out on a date. She said no, several times, but after he asked for a third time she agreed. They went to a movie in a town about ten miles away. It was the first time she had been to a movie in years. She wasn't interested in Joe. Maybe it was because of Homer but she wasn't sure. She just knew how she felt. Joe kissed her good night when they got home from the movies. He called her a few times after that but she always said no. Eventually, he stopped calling.

Hilda began to take a little interest in the house. Due to lack of funds all of the work had to be done by her or the boys. She bough some nice fabric and made some curtains for the windows. The boys put them up for her. For years she had not paid any attention to the fact that she didn't have them. Being private had never been a problem. No one lived close enough to them to see anything. The only people left in the hollow were the Plunks and they couldn't see their house from theirs. None the less, she liked how the curtains looked. They made the place look more homey.

She got some paint from the General Store. The store was changing paint suppliers and she bought it at a very good price. The boys spent the better part of the summer painting and scraping the house. The house must not have been painted in over fifty years. It took two coats of paint but when they were done it looked pretty good. Grandfather had been the supervisor and even he thought they did a good job.

When Billy turned sixteen he got his driver's license. Hilda was pleased with the children. The two older boys were working. All of the children still got their studies done before watching television. The only concern she had was for her grandfather. He wasn't looking well at all. She had called him several times and wanted to go over to his house but he always said he didn't want her to come. He still came out to her place two or three times a week.

---

# *Chapter Eight*

Time was moving on. Hilda realized that she had not seen Homer in several years. Everything was well with the children, almost too well as if something bad was bound to happen. Then she thought that things were just getting even after all the trash she had to tolerate with Homer when they were married.

Billy was in his last year of high school. He was doing well and had talked about going into the army when he graduated. Bobby was in the eleventh grade. Both he and Billy were working in the grocery store in town. Jimmy had taken over the paper route and was in the ninth grade. Kathy was in the seventh grade. She was starting to look like a young lady. She wasn't attractive but she looked nice. Many people had said just that. She looked nice. Kathy didn't like it when they said it. She felt it was like saying you do not look bad. Hilda wasn't sure how to take such remarks, either. She knew in her heart that Kathy could be anything she wanted to be and she told her that on several occasions. She was a straight A student. Not in Jimmy's class but dam smart. When the time came she hoped to get some type of higher education. Hilda thought she would make a good teacher.

In school Jimmy had not changed. Every time

Hilda went to school for him, all of his teachers had good things to say about him. He was an avid reader. When he wasn't in school or working, he was reading something. At times, he would have nine or ten books checked out of the library.

Hilda was concerned that he didn't have much of a social life. She wondered if he was still suffering from the effects of Homer. He was still spending alot of time at the other end of the tunnel. He had gone over there so many times that he could walk through the tunnel without a light. He was now six feet tall. He was going to be a handsome man in a few years. Whenever he and Billy got into an argument, it ended up in a pushing match. Jimmy never hit Billy. He just held him down until he cooled off. He was obviously the stronger of the two. The coaches at the high school wanted him to try out for their teams, but Jimmy showed little interest in sports.

Jimmy had not been around the house for some time. Hilda decided to take a walk through the tunnel and see if he was there. She got a light and headed out from the house. It was the first time she had been back to the tunnel since that first time with Jimmy. Going through it alone made it seem longer. She noticed some stones hanging down from the ceiling and wondered if it were safe. Nothing had fallen to the floor of the tunnel so she figured it must be alright. As she came out on the other side she saw the view and she saw Jimmy sitting on his bench reading. She said hello and asked if she could join him for a little while.

He said, "Sure," and slid over on the bench. They sat there for awhile not saying a word. She was taking in the view and he was reading. Finally he looked at her and said, "You don't mind me coming over here, do you?"

"Not at all. I just came over to see if you were all right and to take another look of this view." She got up to leave and said dinner would be ready in about one hour. He nodded in recognition.

Hardly any time seemed to pass before Billy had enlisted in the army. It broke her heart to see him go, although she knew there was nothing for him in that area. Maybe he could find a better life somewhere else. She prayed that he would. After he left something seemed to be missing in the house. It would take Hilda quite awhile to get used to his absence.

The summer passed quickly and the children were back in school. With Billy gone the child support would be less. Thinking ahead as he usually did the doctor asked Hilda if she could work five days a week. That more than made up for the difference in her income.,

Bobby had made the track team at school as a long distance runner. Weighing in at about one hundred fifty pounds, he had to be in top shape. Before he graduated he would set a state record at his high school. His grades were very good. Bobby had his mother's hair. It was the same dishwater blond. He was just under six feet tall.

Bobby was always working on some project. He was a good planner. He knew where he was and where he wanted to go. When he found out he was going to the academy, he started to do those things that would help him when he got there.

Hilda had received letters from three schools offering to give him a partial scholarship. It broke her heart that she had no way of helping with the balance he would need. Even if it were a full scholarship he would still have to have clothes. He didn't even own a pair of dress shoes or a suit.

She thought about a military school such as West Point. She talked this over with the doctor and he said he would check it out. A short time later Bobby began to receive received a alot of mail, including a letter from his congressman. There were all sorts of forms to fill out. There were things the congressman wanted to know.

After filling out forms, answering questions and sending them back in they heard nothing for three months. Finally a letter came. In her excitement Hilda opened it and read it. Bobby was accepted into the Naval Academy. Hardly believing her eyes, she sat down and cried. When Bobby got home from his job at the store she was still crying. He asked her why? She handed him the letter. After reading it he got down on his knees, put his head in her lap, and they both cried.

Shortly afterward, grandfather came by and shared in the good news. He insisted on having the letter. He took it to town and had three copies made. Then he stopped at the general store, bought three frames and put the letters in them. Coming back to the house, he gave the original back to Bobby. He hung a copy in the house, gave Hilda one for the doctor's office and kept one for himself.

The next day Hilda took the framed copy of the letter to work. She gave it to the doctor and thanked him. She asked him if he would hang it on the wall and he said he would be proud to.

For a few weeks Bobby was the talk of the town. People he hardly knew would approach him at the grocery store and congratulate him. After all the attention stopped he started thinking. Perhaps going to the Naval Academy was just what he wanted to do. From what he heard they weren't giving anything away there. He would have to study as hard as he could and get in top shape. Actually, getting ready for the academy was how he set the state record for long distance running.

The new routine that Bobby had put himself on left little time for a social life. As a matter of fact, he had only one date while going to high school. That was for the prom. After school, running, work and some studying there was hardly enough time left for sleep.

Bobby excelled at math and most of his study time was spent on that subject. He had finished all the math courses at school. One of the teachers was giving him advanced math help.

Jimmy was going to the tunnel often. When he wasn't in school or working most of his time was spent there. It was no longer a complete secret. Bobby and Kathy found out about it but they showed no interest in it. They had all agreed, however, to keep it a family secret.

Jimmy, over the last couple years, had made

improvements to the far end of the tunnel. He had built an overhang at the tunnel entrance. Since the end of the tunnel faced east and most of the rain came out of the west it worked nicely. When there was a light rain he could sit at the entrance without getting wet. Inside the tunnel about twenty feet or so, partially hidden in one of the walls, was a small chest. In the chest he kept a set of field glasses, paper, pencils, books and on occasion, a couple pieces of fruit to stave off hunger between meals.

Down in the valley the individual farms and houses had taken on lives of their own in Jimmy's mind. He had names for most of them. There was a big fancy house that he called The Castle. One farm had a big red barn and was simply called Big Red. There was a large brown farm house that was called Farmer Brown's and so forth.

One day when Jimmy came to the tunnel he was in for a surprise. There on the bench in a plastic bag and being held down by a stone was a note. He opened it and it read, "My name is Carol. I live on a farm down in the valley. I go to school and I am in the tenth grade. The farm where I live is the small white house on the lower left. I have seen you up here a few times. Twice when I have walked up here you were gone. I would like to meet you. If you would agree, leave a note with the time in the plastic bag and I will come."

Jimmy didn't know what to do. He put the note back in the plastic bag and left it. He had trouble keeping his mind on reading. While he was trying to read a plan was taking shape. He put his book away and looked down at the house. It was actually the first house coming into the valley. He had taken orders from the grocery store there a few times but he couldn't remember seeing a girl there.

The next day when he had finished his work at the grocery store Jimmy asked the delivery man if he could ride with him. He said he was off the clock, that he just wanted to get some fresh air. He had noticed that there were some orders to be delivered to the next valley where Carol's white house was. On the way back they ran right past the house. A young girl was in the side yard taking in some laundry from the clothes line. It must have been Carol. Wondering why he hadn't seen her before, he liked what he saw.

Arriving home, he ate quickly and headed for the tunnel. Today, he didn't spend any time reading or looking at the view. He made out a note for Carol suggesting that they plan to meet at the tunnel a week from then. He felt that amount of time might be needed for her to find his note.

To his surprise the very next day when he went back she had answered and agreed to meet him. Jimmy never had a date with a girl. He thought about telling his mother but he decided against it.

When the day came for their meeting he was at the tunnel, early. He got the field glasses out and sat down on the bench. Through the glasses he watched her leave the house and start across the field to the base of the hill. He followed her coming up the hill. The glasses were only put away when she was close enough to him to be able to see he was using them. She was carrying something. As she walked up to him he saw it was a book. At first they just stood there and looked at each other. Without saying so they both liked what they saw. She spoke first.

"I think I have seen you before. You work at the grocery store, don't you?"

"Yes, I do but why haven't I seen you there?"

"Well, my mother does most of our grocery shopping by phone. I have only been to the store a few times."

"Then why haven't I seen you at school?"

"We go to two different schools." Although they lived less than a thousand feet from each other, a mountain separated them and they went to different schools.

She said, "You must come here to study and read, Jimmy." She had brought a book with her and thought they could read it together. It seemed such an ideal place to do just that. He motioned her to sit down on the bench with him.

For awhile, they seemed to want to talk rather than read. She said she had mentioned this place to her father. He said that he had almost forgotten about the tunnel. The farmers from their valley had built it there more than a hundred years ago. Originally, it was intended for water for the homes and farms in the valley. The creek that was in the hollow was dammed up and the water was piped through the tunnel. Since it was alot higher than the valley floor they didn't need any pumps.

Over the years the people who owned the hollow sold their mineral rights for the coal and several mines opened up. The mines run off destroyed the water and the system was no longer used. Someone had sold the pipes and valves for scrap.

That answered alot of questions that Jimmy had thought about since finding the tunnel.

They talked for about an hour before Carol said she had to get back. When she left Jimmy told her she was welcome back anytime and he would look forward to seeing her again. She didn't answer but she smiled and he knew she would be back. In a short period of time they were meeting at the tunnel two or three times a week. She was doing her homework there and Jimmy was reading and just enjoying being with her. Any school problem she had Jimmy would help her with. She was impressed with his knowledge and found it hard to believe he was in the same grade as she was. Jimmy's height was apt to fool one, too. At six feet three inches tall, he looked like he should be in a higher grade. The next day Carol called Jimmy's school as if she was checking for a job reference. Now she believed he was in the tenth grade.

As time went on they spent more and more time together. They liked being together alot. They even kissed a couple of times as they were parting at the tunnel. Jimmy was confused as he was having feelings that he had never had before. He really liked Carol but with his new feelings, he wasn't sure how he should treat her.

Jimmy called the doctor. He didn't want to talk about this with his mother. The doctor saw him one afternoon when his appointments were over. At first Jimmy was a little slow getting started. Then it all came out.

"Doc," he said, "I like Carol very much. I don't to do anything to hurt her but sometimes I find myself wanting her real bad. What should I do, Doc? What is the right thing to do?"

"Jimmy, you always treat a person the way you would like to be treated. Not just a person but all people."

Jimmy said, "but I am just talking about Carol."

"Are you? If you are going to treat all people the way you would like to be treated then what about her father? If you had a young daughter would you like someone to have sex with her before they were married? What about her mother? What about your mother? Would you like to tell your mother that at fifteen you were having sex with a young girl? Or would you be prepared to tell your mother that she was expecting a baby? Which of these things do you think is the best?"

With that Jimmy had one more question. Carol had said she was a Catholic. He said that he had heard nothing of Catholics but thought he should learn more about them. How could he do this? The doctor reached back to a stand behind his desk. He got a Bible and handed it to him. He said, "This will be a good place to start. I will see if I can get you some other books as well."

After the first visit to the doctor, Jimmy took a serious look at what he said. For several weeks he read the Bible. He also went over the other books that he had received. He and Carol talked about the things that he and Dr. Rhodes had discussed. She had fallen in love with

Jimmy as well and they decided to limit their personal contact to kissing.

---

# *Chapter Nine*

The year passed without much more happening.
Bobby's time to go to the academy had come. He had been
getting things ready for a couple weeks. Jimmy kidded
him by saying they were supposed to take care of everything at the academy. Bobby looked like he was moving
there not just going there.

The people at the grocery store had a going away
party for him. There were about fifty people there. The
doctor attended. Even Carol and her parents came.
Everybody chipped in and bought him luggage as a going
away present. Hilda was down in the dumps about his
leaving. As with Billy, it would take her some time to get
over his being away from home.

A couple of months after Bobby left, Billy came
home. He was on leave for thirty days. Hilda enjoyed his
being there as did the rest of the family. She mothered him
more then than she had before he left. He was nineteen.
He had found a girl in Alabama and he was talking about
marriage when he got back from going overseas. That's
how Hilda learned that he was going to war in the far east.
With that news she felt so sick that she had to lay down
for awhile. After she got up Billy hit her with the rest of
the bad news. He was going to spend the last week of his

leave with his girlfriend and her family in Alabama.

As he was leaving he said, "Mom, I love you. I did not want tell you about going overseas because I wanted to enjoy this time with you and not have you worrying." He hugged her and left.

While Billy had been away he wrote home every other week. Hilda got accustomed to receiving his letters and hoped he would continue to write home while he was overseas.

It was 1969. The war was going on strong. Billy's letters came as expected. From his letters you would have thought he was off on an extended vacation. He wrote that he had been promoted to sergeant. Then Hilda received the letter that is every mother's nightmare. Billy had been killed. She read it over and over. She didn't want to believe it.

A few days went by and she hadn't left the house. Mrs. Plunk had come over but Hilda couldn't bring herself to get out of bed. Several of the towns people had dropped off food items. She had no interest in anything. Finally, the doctor made his second visit. This time he came not just as friend but a doctor. He was beginning to get concerned about her health. They talked for awhile and he told her that the other children needed her. He gave her a shot and some medication. Shortly after he left she got out of bed.

Hilda was barely getting back on her feet when she was notified that Billy's body would be coming home in about ten days. He earned a silver star for bravery. She had to ask what that was. There were funeral arrangements to be made. She didn't have a plot at the cemetery for him. Here the doctor had been ahead of her. When the towns people heard about the silver star they got together and arranged for a family area, consisting of six plots, to be made available to Hilda.

Hilda had finally heard from Homer. He had not come by the house nor talked to the children since their divorce. He had heard about Billy's death and his winning the silver star. He said Billy was a Willow and should be buried in the Willow family plot. Hilda said, "There is no way in hell that's going to happen."

He said, "By God, he would be out to talk some sense into her."

Hilda mentioned this to Kathy and Jimmy when they got home from school. She had never seen Jimmy get mad before but he was cooking now. He went outside and sat by the front of the house. About twenty minutes later Homer drove up. He parked in front of the house. He got out of the truck and headed straight for the kitchen door. Jimmy stood in his way. He said, "What do you want, boy?" Homer tried to push him aside. He realized he couldn't. Jimmy said, "Get back in your truck and leave." Homer said, "Screw you, boy."

As this was happening Kathy and Hilda were watching from the window. From the time he had driven up all Jimmy could remember was being tied to that tree. With Homer's last remark Jimmy hit him just once. It was full in the face. Homer had a look of disbelief on his face. Then he just fell over. He was out cold.

Jimmy picked him up by the belt with one arm. He carried him over and put him in the back of the truck . He then got in the truck and drove it to the end of the dirt road. He noticed a pencil and paper on the front seat of the truck. He wrote Homer a short note and pinned it to his shirt. It simply said, "Don't come back. The next time I will use a belt on you like you did on me."

When Jimmy walked back to the house they were waiting. One by one they gave him a hug. Hilda said, It's good to have a real man around the house."

Services were held for Billy. They were very nice indeed. Bobby came home from the service. He looked so handsome in his white uniform. Most of the town was there. Homer was no where to be found. The town had purchased a head stone for Billy. It had a soldier carved on it with a flag. It had his name, the usual dates, his rank and a silver star.

It took Hilda about a month to start getting back to her old self. She could not accept the fact that Billy was gone.

Jimmy took the test and got his driver's license. He only used the car about twice a month to take Carol to the movies or to some function at school. Other than that he would run an occasional errand for his mother.

Grandfather had taught him how to change the oil. In the four years that they had the car they had not put many miles on it. The car was now eight years old and still only had twenty-five thousand miles.

Jimmy and Carol still spent quite a bit of time at

the end of the tunnel. One of the reasons Carol's family didn't mind her going there was that her grades had gone from C's to A's. They had also met Jimmy and they were fond of him.

They were about to start the last year of high school. They had been dating for almost two years. They said they were going steady for one year but neither of them had dated anyone before. At the end of the tunnel they had taken kissing to a new high. But that was it, just kissing. They talked about the future but nothing seemed to look very good. Jimmy thought he might just go into the service like his brothers or just kick around and wait to be drafted.

Hilda started to get mail from several schools. With his grades and scores in high school they were offering him everything but the kitchen sink. Some of the offers even included a monthly spending allowance. All of this seemed to confuse Jimmy all the more. He decided to do what he always did, he went to see the doctor when he has had a problem. He asked Jimmy what he would like to do and he said most everything.

"No," the doctor said. "What would you like to do for the rest of your life?"

"I'm not sure."

"Well, you will just have to give it some thought." He told Jimmy he wanted to see him the following week to discuss what ideas he came up with.

That was a tough week for Jimmy. He spent all of his spare time going over in his head what the doctor had said. The week went by slowly but by the end of it he was ready for his meeting with the doctor. When he was asked what he wanted to be he said, "A doctor just like you."

"I was hoping you would say that. But is it really what you want?"

"Yes it is, I have made up my mind."

"Well, that's just fine. I have been doing some checking for you. I didn't know that you had a perfect 4.0 grade average."

"Doctor, I haven't taken regular high school classes for the last year."

The doctor contacted the school he had attended and after talking to them and telling them about Jimmy, they not on only offered him a full ride scholarship but they wanted him to come up to the college for a week to be evaluated for placement.

Jimmy asked the doctor what that meant and he wasn't sure.

The date for the senior prom was still a couple of months away. Jimmy asked Carol if she would go with him. She said yes. Jimmy began to realize that he had some things to do to get himself ready for the prom. He mentioned his problem to Mr. Welch. He told Jimmy he had a tuxedo that he hadn't used in some time. He was welcome to it if he wanted it. He went to Mr. Welch's house and tried it on. It would need a little altering but Jimmy felt it looked pretty good.

He talked to Hilda. She agreed to buy him a shirt, shoes and a tie. He had enough time to save the money he would need for the other items such as prom tickets, food after the prom and Carol's corsage.

Transportation was the last hang up. Jimmy was at Carol's one night when they were going over their plans. There was no place to rent a car or hire a limo in the area.

Carol's father overheard their conversation. He said they were welcome to use their family car if it would help. That put the last piece of the puzzle together.

There wasn't a place in Franklin to buy a gown. Carol and her mother spent a whole day traveling to the state capitol to buy her one. Jimmy asked her what it looked like? She said you will like it but that was all she would tell him.

Jimmy picked up his altered tuxedo and took it to the cleaners for a final pressing. Everything was all set. He got dressed and left in Hilda's car to drive over to Carol's to switch cars and pick her up.

When he got there he was invited into the house. Carol came down just after he got there. She was beautiful in that gown. He could not keep his eyes off of her. He gave her the corsage. Her parents wanted to take a few pictures. This being done, they were on their way.

In the car Carol slid over close to Jimmy. He said, "God, Carol, you look great tonight." She said she wanted to look great, tonight, just for him.

When they arrived at the dance Jimmy realized this was the first time many of his friends from school had ever seen Carol. Most of the girls in the school didn't expect Jimmy to even come to the prom as he had never dated a girl from that school the entire time he went there.

They were the center of attraction for most of the night. As with most things that are enjoyable, it ended too soon.

After the dance they went down to the valley to a restaurant for a late meal. They were home at her door by one o'clock. That was the agreed upon time. They had a longer than usual good night kiss. He gave Carol the keys to the car and he drove home. Going home he thought of how wonderful Carol was. This had been the most enjoyable night of his life.

Mr. Welch's wife had died a few years ago. He was in his mid forties and still in pretty good shape. He had been out with Hilda a few times and they seemed to hit it off rather well. He had even taken a sincere interest in Kathy and Jimmy. He had talked to Jimmy many times and they both enjoyed the conversations. He asked Jimmy what he thought about him and his mother getting married. Jimmy in his practical manner said, "That would be fine with me but don't you think you should be asking her?" They both had a laugh. Then he said that he had already asked her and she was thinking about it.

Bob was the type of lawyer one hopes he can get but seldom does. He was of average height and weight. He had a smile that lit up the room. Everyone liked him. He had a manner that put people at ease. He talked with you not to you. You knew, somehow, that you could depend on him. Simply put, he liked people and they liked him.

The college sent Jimmy a letter. They wanted him

to come up to be evaluated in two weeks. He showed the letter to Hilda and the doctor. He would be needing a few things, some new clothes for a starter. The doctor took him to the store and bought him a complete outfit. Bobby had sent home the luggage he received because it didn't fit into his needs in the Navy. Jimmy could use it.

Mr. Welch had him come by his place. They were about the same size. They went into his closet and they selected two outfits. They went to the tailor's and had them altered. After that it was on to the store for some shirts, ties, socks, underwear and another pair of shoes. Jimmy couldn't thank him enough. He wondered if this was to impress Hilda. Jimmy didn't care because he really wanted her to say yes, anyway.

Jimmy had been keeping Carol up to date on what was happening. She was also excited. The day before he was to leave Carol came over and helped him pack. They hoped with all their hearts that this would work out like they thought it should.

The day of departure came and Jimmy arrived early at the bus station. His bus was due at seven and he was there waiting at six-twenty. His Mom and Kathy had left and Carol stayed and waited with him. When the bus came they hugged, kissed and said goodbye. Carol was crying as if he was leaving forever.

Soon the bus was out of the valley. It was almost a three hundred mile trip to the college. Jimmy sat on a window seat. The bus was only half full. He had never been out of the valley before. As he looked out the window he was engrossed in the scenery. The more he saw, the smaller and smaller he felt. Because of his interest in new and unknown, the time seemed to fly by.

Fortunately, the bus dropped him off right in front of the college. He had been told to report to the administration building. He saw the signs and he proceeded. As he got to the door an older man came out and held it for him to go in with his bag. This man introduced himself. He was the president of the college and he had been waiting for him.

He took Jimmy into his office where he asked him several questions. How things were in school? How old was he and so forth? He mentioned Dr. Rhodes and asked how he was. They had worked together several years ago and they were still good friends. Jimmy liked the man. He seemed easy to talk to. They went on this way for almost an hour. Then, he took Jimmy outside to his car and drove him to the dormitory where he would be staying.

A young man by the name of Simon met them at the door. He was assigned to show Jimmy the ropes while he was there.

President Roberts left and Simon helped Jimmy to his room. The room looked like it held three people but he was the only one in it. Simon suggested that he unpack. He would be back in a little while to take him to dinner.

After dinner Jimmy went back to his room. He wanted to get a good night's sleep but he was having a hard time. His mind kept going over all the new things he had seen that day just getting there and what they had discussed in the office. It seemed like he lay there awake for hours. He hoped he could get some sleep before his ten a.m. meeting. Sleep finally came.

The next morning he was back in the office with Mr. Roberts. A few minutes later, another man came in. He was introduced as the head of a department at the school. Jimmy did not hear what department. He was told that he would spend the day with five different department heads. He left the office, shortly thereafter, to meet the first. The meeting was like the others would be. Many questions, then some testing and evaluations.

After the fifth day, which was a short day, they all met back in Dr. Roberts office. They were all pleased with the time they had spent with Jimmy. A study plan had been put together and he was presented with several books. They wanted him to study these books and know them cover to cover when he came back the next fall.

Jimmy thanked them. The following morning he was back on the bus heading home.

The day after he got home, he went to see the doctor. He brought the books with him. He was confused. The doctor had been in touch with Dr. Roberts. They had been very impressed with him, so much that if he could cover the material they had given him, they would start him off in the second year. What the doctor didn't tell him was that they believed he was one of the brightest applicants that had ever applied to that school.

With the extra study work Jimmy was doing, he was seeing less of Carol. She didn't seem to mind, she understood. They still found time to read, study and kiss at the tunnel.

Two big things happened during Jimmy's last year in school. First, Grandfather died. It was not unexpected but it hurt nonetheless. He almost made it to eighty. He had said he hoped he would. To Hilda's surprise he had left instructions to be cremated. She wondered why. She talked to the undertaker and he told her that he had his services all paid for. Then a few months ago he came in and had them changed. He said he needed a refund for the difference.

"How much was that?" asked Hilda.

He said about fifteen hundred dollars.

She said, "Oh, Grandfather," and she turned away. She remembered he had given her that amount for Kathy's braces.

Grandfather had his house and an older pickup truck. This was given to Hilda. They looked at his house and it had the bare minimum of furniture. Hilda knew why. With what furniture he had and what they had, it would make do nicely. Grandfather's house was downtown. It was much newer and nicer. They decided to move.

The second big thing was that Hilda said yes to Mr. Welch. They set the date for a couple of months later,

Mr. Welch knew about the planned move and the house. He suggested they put off the move until he could get the house painted inside and out and have the carpet changed. He wanted this to be his wedding present to the family. It was agreed upon.

As it turned out he did more than that. He built a free standing three car garage. Then he converted the two car attached garage into an office. He then traded Hilda's old car and Grandfather's truck in on a new Mercury as a wedding present for Hilda.

Everything was moved into the house just before the wedding. Almost the entire town attended. Jimmy and Kathy did the final touches to the house while Hilda was on her honeymoon.

# *Chapter Ten*

Jimmy's last year in high school went by quickly as expected. He graduated number one in his class. In the fall he would be off to college. Kathy would be starting in the eleventh grade. Bobby would be in his third year in the academy. He was doing very well and was in the top five in his class. He managed to get home for most of the summer. They all enjoyed being together. Mr. Welch, or as he was now called Bob, fit well into the family group..

Bob wanted Hilda to stop working at the clinic but she decided not to. She liked the independence that she felt it gave her. The doctor promoted her to receptionist. Now she mainly answered the phone and made appointments. The job also required some filing and light paperwork. She picked it up quickly and liked it.

Hilda and Bob hit it off great. For the first time she had a man who really cared for her. Being with him at night was such a joy. Now she realized how much she had missed all those years being married to Homer. More often than not they looked like a couple of teenagers when they took their nightly walk after dinner.

Shortly after they moved from the hollow the house burned down. No one knew what caused it. Homer was planning to move in but he would have to make other plans now.

One evening Hilda drove out and parked by the homesite. She just sat there awhile and drove back.

The Plunks also moved from the hollow. They were the last family to move. Now there was no one living there. At one time, several years ago, there had been more than twenty families living there.

After they moved Jimmy missed using the tunnel. It didn't affect his studying much as he had a room of his own at their new house. Most of his studying was from books they had given him at college. Once or twice he needed help from Doctor Rhodes. He really liked the material and he applied himself until he mastered it.

During the last year it was nice for Jimmy to have a man around the house to talk to. He and Bob spent many hours together. Bob helped Jimmy gain prospective in many ways. They came to be very close friends.

Jimmy worked his last summer at the grocery store. Since he had graduated from high school they had let him work full time. This helped him put aside money for school. He saved most of the money that he made.

Jimmy was seeing Carol almost every night after work. They usually took in a movie or went for a short ride in the car and parked. They had become very close but the rule of kissing only held fast. Jimmy could not believe how much he loved her. She said she felt the same way.

It was time for Jimmy to go off to college. He had been preparing for weeks. That morning once again they said their goodbyes at the bus station and he was off. It was the fall of 1971 and he was about to do something he had only dreamed of.

They had asked him to come to school a week early. He met with the department heads he had met the last time. He was with each one for a day and then, they met as a group at the end. They went over his high school studies and the additional work they had given him. He had taken four years of Latin in high school. They were in total agreement. Jimmy would be starting in his second year of college this fall.

It took nearly two months for Jimmy to adjust to his new life style and study routine. After that things were as usual, he was right at the top of his class.

He and Carol had been exchanging letters about once a week. In the winter the tone of her letters seemed to change. Then there were fewer, then they stopped all together. Jimmy was about to go crazy. He had called her home a few times but she was never there when he called. At least that's what they said. He still had three weeks to go before he would be going home for the summer. He didn't have the money to make the trip any sooner. He decided to call the doctor. The doctor said he hadn't heard anything about Carol but he would check it out and get back to him. A couple days later he called to say was that all he found out was that Carol had gone out of town. He didn't know why but he thought it might have been for work as there was none, locally. She had been gone for about three months.

Jimmy wondered what he had done or said. He went back over the letters he had written but couldn't find anything. This weighed heavily on his mind as the last few days of school ground down.

Jimmy headed home. When he got off the bus he went home dropped his bags off, got in his mother's car and drove straight over to Carol's. He knocked on the door. Her father came out and closed the door behind him. He was face to face with Jimmy on the porch. Jimmy asked him where Carol was. He said that she was out of state but he could not tell him where. He asked if there was some way he could get in touch with her. He told him, no.

Jimmy said, "Sir, have I done something wrong?"

He said, "No, son, you have done nothing wrong."

These words caused a flash back. Jimmy suddenly remembered asking his mother what he had done wrong to have his father beat him so. He started to turn and leave. It was then that he noticed a tear on the man's cheek. Her father stopped him and said "Carol got herself in a family way and went out of the state to have the baby."

Jimmy said, "I didn't do it."

He said, "I know."

As Jimmy was leaving he said, "God, I wish I was the father."

As he left he felt that someone had cut his gut out. By the time he got home he was exhausted. He went straight to his room and slept through the night. He had never done that before. The long hours of studying for finals, then the trip home and the problem had been a bit much.

The next day he went to see the doctor. He told him about Carol. Then he asked the doctor what he had done wrong?

"Well," the doctor said, "it is hard enough for you to do what is right. Then you have to depend on other people to do the same to you. That doesn't always happen. We cannot always be responsible for what other people do."

"But I loved her. I thought she loved me."

"What's to say she didn't? People change. There may be a reason or maybe not. You, my son, have to let it go."

"I know," Jimmy said.

This was the first time anyone had seen Jimmy cry.

The doctor looking at the boy said, "Jimmy, the world turns only one way. A day passes with each turn. You can't turn it back. What has happened in the past you cannot change. You have to accept it as fact. Adjust your life and go on."

"Doctor, have you ever been in love?"

He answered, "It would be hard to go through life and not fall in love but today we are discussing your problem."

It just wasn't the same for Jimmy being home without Carol. One afternoon he went up to the tunnel. Looking down at her house he just couldn't stay there.

He was working half time for the doctor and half time for Bob doing odd jobs for his law office. He got twenty dollars a week. This was for his spending money. When it was time for him to go back to school they each would give him the balance for his school needs.

They kept him pretty busy. With Carol not being there he wasn't spending much of his pocket money. For the first month he just seemed to be going through the motions. Then Bobby came home for two weeks. His navy commitment required him to spend most of the summer with them. Bobby and Jimmy spent almost two weeks together. This took his mind off of Carol, somewhat..

Bobby would be in his last year at the academy. He had done very well. They asked him to go on to graduate school and study nuclear physics. He had agreed so upon completion of his four years at the academy he would be going to M.I.T. He asked Jimmy, "Could you have thought just a few years ago that I would be going to M.I.T. and you would be in pre-med?"

Bobby had become a man. You could tell by the way he talked. Now people wanted to be around him and they listened to what he had to say. Hilda mentioned that very thing to Bob. He agreed and said that was an early sign of leadership. He had not known Bobby as well as the others. He was impressed with what he saw and said that the navy was dam lucky to be getting such a man.

With Bobby back to the service and the summer almost half gone Jimmy started looking forward to going back to school. Carol still came to his mind from time to time. He wondered how she was and where she was. He knew in his heart it was over for them. Still he felt he would like to talk to her one more time to find out what the had gone wrong.

Jimmy met a high school classmate who went to work for the post office after school. He ran into him at the doctor's office. They talked for awhile and the subject of Carol came up. Jimmy told him what happened and he was surprised. Jimmy said he would like to get in touch with her one more time but he didn't know how. The friend said he might be able to help. He would check things out and get back to him.

After checking the mail going to Carol's house for about a week, it came. A letter from Carol with a return address. The address was given to Jimmy with the under-standing that no one would ever find out where it came from.

That evening Jimmy wrote her a letter. When he finished he read it. Then he tore it up and started over. He realized the first letter was about his hurt and problems with what had happened. If she was expecting a baby she had enough problems. He just sent her a letter that said he felt sorry for her and wished there was some way he could have helped. It was still two weeks until he had to go back to school an he hoped he would get an answer.

The doctor was having a birthday. Hilda found out it was his birthday when he received a card from out of town. Bob and Hilda invited him over to their house for dinner. When the he got there he was delighted to see that they had planned a small party with a cake!

After dinner as they sat at the table and talked. All

those who were present thought the world of Dr. Rhodes. but it occurred to them that they knew very little about him. This was his sixtieth year. He had come to town just out of school. He had been there all those years and no one knew where he was from.

The good doctor started to get several questions and he didn't seem to mind. Where did he go to medical school? Jimmy answered that question. Where was he from? He said he was born and raised just outside of the Washington D.C. area. His father was in the construction business. He had one older brother who went to college and received a degree in engineering. After school he went to work in the family business and had done very well. His mother and father were both gone. The birthday card had come from his brother and his wife.

"How did you decide to become a doctor?" Hilda asked.

"Well, that's hard to say. When I started school I wasn't sure what I wanted to do. Once I even thought of becoming a priest. A girl I met my first year in school let me know that being a priest was not for me. I've always liked helping and working with people. Being a doctor seemed the best way to do that."

"What happened to the girl?" Jimmy asked.

"Goodness, that was over forty years ago. I don't even remember her name."

Jimmy wondered if she was the doctor's one big love.

"Why didn't you ever get married?"

"That's a good question. As a matter of fact I have thought of that myself many times. I guess there was just not enough time. When I came here there was no doctor in the area. The work load was such, at first, that I never even considered it. Then later, I felt I was too old. What I really wanted was to have children. I consider almost everyone under the age of 35 in this town to be one of my children. Look at it this way. I was there when they were born. When they were sick I was there to help them. Then as they grew I prayed to the Lord that they would be well and grow up to be good people. Isn't that kind of what a parent does?"

Jimmy listened to it all. He wondered if the people in that room and the people in that town really knew how much that man had meant to them all. Jimmy looked at him differently now. He realized fully what he had done for him. He had been his father just like he said.

The man that turned sixty looked sixty. Soon he would have to slow down. Jimmy wondered what they would do without him.

Kathy was starting her last year in high school. As the others before her she had always made good grades. She wondered what she might do after she graduated. She had thought of becoming a nurse but she wasn't sure. She had talked to Hilda and Bob but nothing was firm.

Homer made the local news. He had beaten up on his eight year old son then turned on his wife. She wasn't the forgiving type like Hilda. She preferred charges against him. He had the nerve to ask Bob to defend him.

Before it went to trial it was settled out of court. He agreed to give her a divorce, pay child support and alimony. It was to be taken right out of his pay check like before.

When Bob married Hilda he wanted to have all the ties to Homer broken. He adopted Kathy. By doing so he relieved Homer of his last two years of child support. When she read about Homer in the newspaper, Hilda laughed and said it looked like he was back at it again.

Just before Jimmy was to go back to school Hilda found out she was pregnant. She and Bob were very happy. She was having her first child in seventeen years. That seemed like a long time. It was, but she was still only thirty eight years old.

When Jimmy left for school this time there were no tears. Hilda kissed him goodbye at the house. He got into his two year old Volkswagen Bug and drove off. Bob had taken the car as payment for some of his services. He had given it to Jimmy. It wasn't much but it fit right in at college. More important, it got you from point A to point B much quicker.

This year Jimmy would be starting his third year of studies, although it was still his second year at school. He had gotten a job at the school library. It wasn't much of a job but it paid by the hour. He worked twenty hours a week. In truth it was like a study hall as most students knew what they wanted and signed out the books themselves. He took his studies with him and got most of his homework done while he was getting paid.

Many of the students in his class asked Jimmy for help when they picked up books from the library. At times, he would spend as much as half an hour with one student. This gave him an idea. If he charged for tutoring he could make some extra money.

Before he started tutoring he decided to get Dr. Roberts opinion. He made an appointment and went to his office. He told him what he had in mind. Dr. Roberts asked him how much he was paying to go to school? He said nothing. Well then, don't you think you owe the school something for what it has given you?"

Jimmy said, "I guess I do."

"Well then, are you being paid for your time in the library?"

"Yes, I am."

"Well, what's your problem? If you were running the school who would you put in the library? Your dumbest or smartest student? Jimmy, you are being helped. Don't you think you should help some others as well if you can?"

After Jimmy left his office he knew Dr. Roberts was right and he also knew he had grown a little that day.

Jimmy hadn't heard from Carol since he sent her that letter. He had phoned home a few times but nothing had come in the mail. He still had her address. He wrote her a letter much like the last and asked her to answer. Then he gave her his address at college. As with the first attempt he got no reply. After a few weeks he thought of sending another letter but with additional reflection he decided to let it be. He felt very strongly about Carol but if this was what she wanted and it sure sounded like it was, then he must just let go.

Everyone was able to get home for the holidays. Hilda was showing her family condition but she managed to get most of the preparations for the holiday done herself.

Everyone was doing well in school. It was nice getting up to speed on what everyone was doing.

Bobby said that he wouldn't be home that next summer. He was going straight from the academy to M.I.T. where he would be taking some summer classes to get a head start.

Kathy had decided to go into nurse's training. Hilda and Bob had been checking out different places to see what they could find for her. They had narrowed it down to one in a small town in Western Pennsylvania or one in Pittsburgh. Everyone was leaning toward the small town.

Shortly after Jimmy got back to school he got a phone call from Bob. He said that Hilda had a miscarriage. It had been a hard one. She was stable but if things turned for the worse he would keep them posted.

Jimmy didn't know what to do. It was Friday and he was about to have his last class. He asked to be excused and he was. He was on the road in twenty minutes. It was a six hour drive in a car but alot faster than a bus with no stops.

When he got home Hilda was still in the clinic but

it was too late to visit her. He went home and about an hour later, Bobby arrived. He had obtained a seventy-two hour pass.

The next day they were able to see her. She seemed very tired and weak. The doctor said she had lost a great deal of blood. He didn't think he would have to give her anymore blood and in a few days, she probably could go home. Hilda had a close call but she would be alright.

At dinner that night Bob filled them in on what happened. It was Thursday evening. Hilda wasn't feeling well. She had gone down to the kitchen about three a.m. to get something to drink. Bob didn't hear a sound. When he found her three hours later she was out cold in the kitchen in a puddle of blood. At first he thought she was dead. He called the doctor. In a few minutes he was there. Hilda had already lost the baby. They picked her up and took her to the clinic. There were other complications. They had to operate. Because of this Hilda would not be able to have anymore children. She did not know this yet. Bob asked them not to tell her now.

Sunday afternoon Jimmy and Bobby visited Hilda. She was looking somewhat better. She thanked them for coming. It looked like she would be alright. They kissed her and as they were leaving she was already falling asleep.

Back at school again Jimmy got into the routine. Time was sliding by. Carol hadn't popped into his mind for some time.

One day he got a call from Bob. He said he wanted

to talk. For a moment he thought something was wrong at home again. This wasn't the case. Bob went on for the better part of an hour. Jimmy said very little. It seemed that fate had raised its head again. Bob said it was Hilda who wanted a baby. He was willing to do anything that made her happy. After she found out that she couldn't have anymore babies she really got depressed. They had talked about adopting. He had her pretty convinced that at his age, which was now close to fifty, that getting a baby through normal channels might be hard to do. She had said she wouldn't mind if it was an older child.

Bob said, "You know what a natural mother she is. She just wants to do what she does best, I guess. Well, here is the problem. Homer has given up all rights to his nine year old son. The boy's mother who has turned out to be just as bad, found another man that she wants to marry. This new fellow wants nothing to do with the boy. She wants to give him up and your mother wants him. What do you think?"

Jimmy was taken back for awhile then he answered. "I probably know how that boy feels more than most. I was about his age when Homer left us. But it's really more important how you two feel."

"I couldn't love her more for being who she is. It shouldn't be a shock to anyone that she wants to do this."

"It's a hard decision for the two of you to make. You can be sure that whatever you decide, I will be one hundred percent with you."

After Bob hung up Jimmy thought about it. He had

never thought much about the boy in the past. He had never looked at him as his half brother but that was what he was. If they adopted him he would have a much better chance to get to know him. The boy would have a much better chance at life. He hoped they would go ahead with the adoption.

Things were picking up at the library. A very attractive second year student was spending alot of time there. She and Jimmy became acquainted and they went out on a few dates. She couldn't understand why Jimmy didn't just take her anywhere she wanted to go. They were flying on different wave lengths and it didn't last long. After it was over, Jimmy just dug deeper on his school work.

Another year was over. It did not seem possible. Jimmy was at the top of his class. Some of the professors told him he needed to be thinking about what branch of medicine he wanted to specialize in. Most thought their field was the best. Jimmy had not given it much thought.

As he drove home he was sorry that he wouldn't be seeing Bobby. He wondered what Hilda and Bob had decided to do about the boy.

When he drove up to the house there was a young boy sitting on the front steps. He looked lost. Jimmy asked him who he was? He said his name was Mike. He asked him if he knew who he was? The boy said he didn't know. Jimmy reached down, picked him up off his feet and hugged him. He said, "I'm your big brother, Jimmy. Mike looked a little shocked. Jimmy put him down. He put his arm around him and they walked into the house.

Hilda was home. She looked better than the last time he saw her. She wanted him to fill her in on his schooling. Then she changed her mind. She said hold off on that. "I see you have met your brother. Is that alright with you?"

"You know dam well it is."

She smiled and said that the reason she didn't want to hear about school was that they were going to have a big dinner that night. Sort of a home coming. Bobby was going to be there for the weekend. She wanted to hear from everyone during and after dinner.

Jimmy was busy taking final exams when Bobby graduated. He said he was sorry he missed it. He asked Hilda how it was. She said it was great! Dr. Rhodes went with her and Bob. They had taken many pictures and they would show them that evening.

Jimmy went to his room and unpacked. He wanted to spend some time with Mike. He planned on taking him swimming several times during the summer. He was glad that Bobby was going to be there. He was looking forward to having a talk with him.

Jimmy and Mike helped Hilda get ready for dinner. It would be just their family and Dr. Rhodes. Everything was ready and everybody was there except Bobby. He had called and said he would be there in thirty minutes. When he arrived he had brought a friend. She was a very attractive lady named Susan. They set another plate at the table and dinner started.

Bobby said that he and Susan had been dating for quite some time and he had brought her home to meet the family. She seemed to fit into the group well.

There wasn't much talk at dinner. Maybe it was because Susan was there. After dinner Susan got up and helped Hilda clear the table. They brought out Hilda's famous carrot cake and coffee. Susan blended in just like she had been in the family for years.

The conversation started. Bobby said he wanted to go first. He had an announcement to make. He and Susan were going to get engaged. She had one more year left in school to get her teaching degree. Shortly after that they planned to get married. Everyone was truly happy for them. Hilda cried a little and Susan jokingly said, "I didn't think I was that bad." Hilda gave her a big hug and welcomed her into the family.

Bobby went on to say that he would be going to M.I.T. for both his masters and doctor's degree. He wasn't sure how long that would take but he felt the navy would want him to go year round. That might cut down some on the time he could come home.

Bobby had graduated from the academy fourth in his class. When you consider that you have to be a straight A student to get into the academy that was quite an accomplishment. Jimmy thought he looked great in his white uniform. With the work he had done at the academy he had filled out nicely and it showed. Jimmy decided that he could do something along those lines and build his own body up a little.

Susan was next. She got the twenty question treatment. She said she was from Pittsburgh. Her last name was Dolan. She was one hundred percent Irish. Her father worked in the steel mills. Her mother worked in an office. An only child, she would be the first in their family to graduate from college. This was her parent's dream and she didn't intend to let them down.

Bob spoke for the first time that evening. He said that the more he heard about Susan the more he liked her. He got up to get more coffee and gave Susan a kiss on the cheek. When Susan first came into the house she felt like she belonged. That kiss was like her official acceptance.

Jimmy was next. He said there wasn't much to tell. He would finish his four years next year. He had been told that he would be accepted to stay there to complete his training. It would be a total of five or six years until he was out on his own. It could be more depending on the field he chose. He hadn't made up his mind on just what that might be. He ranked number one in his class. When he said that, he raised his voice and looked at Bobby who was giving him the finger.

Jimmy said he and Mike were going swimming tomorrow and asked if anyone else wanted to go along. There was no reply. Later Susan and Bobby said that they would come along.

Kathy had been waiting for her turn. She said that she had been accepted into nurses training. She would be starting in the fall. She was looking forward to it as it would be her first trip to stay away from home. With a laugh she said the high school was still figuring out the student grades so she couldn't announce officially her very high ranking. In truth she was in the top ten percent of her class although she was never known to study very hard.

They broke up for the night. The house had only three bedrooms so the boys stayed in one and the girls stayed in the another.

After breakfast everyone had an errand or two to run. Then they loaded up in Hilda's car and the four of them headed off for a swim. There was a large public pool about fifteen miles down the highway. It was a bright, warm, sunny day when they got there about noon.

They went into the locker room to change clothes. When they came out both Mike and Jimmy had tee shirts on with their swimming trunks. Bobby didn't say anything but he knew why Jimmy had his on. For three hours they alternated between swimming and just laying in the sun.

They were about to leave when of all people, Homer showed up. He went over and started talking to Mike. You couldn't hear what they were saying but by their manner they were having an argument. Jimmy walked over in their direction. Homer didn't even notice who he was. About the time he got next to them Homer slapped Mike on the face real hard. As he reached back to slap him again Jimmy grabbed his arm. With almost a reflex action he reached over and grabbed Homer by the neck with his other hand. Jimmy was much bigger than Homer so his hand went almost completely around his neck. In this position with Homer's feet almost off the ground, Jimmy walked him over to his pickup truck. Bobby noticed saw what was happening and he came over with Susan. He asked Jimmy to let him go, more for Jimmy's sake than Homer's. While Jimmy still held him by the neck, Homer told him to go to hell and spit in his face. Bobby had opened the truck door thinking Jimmy was just going to put him in. When he spit on him almost by reflex action Jimmy banged his head against the door jam. Homer was out. They sat him on the front seat and walked back to the pool.

Susan had watched the whole thing and in a state of shock, she said, "What in the hell was that all about?"

Jimmy said, "Rather than tell you, let me show you." He turned Mike around and said, "Why do you think he had his tee shirt on?" With that he lifted it up. When Susan saw Mike's back she had to turn away.

On the ride back from swimming Mike told Susan who Homer was. She said she didn't like people acting that way.

Jimmy said, "did you notice that I was wearing a tee shirt, also?" Nothing more was said about the matter.

Except for that incident at the swimming pool the weekend was great. Monday came and Bobby and Susan left early. It was always great to see Bobby and they were all pleased that he had found someone as nice as Susan.

---

# *Chapter Eleven*

Jimmy and Kathy settled into the summer routine. She had a job at the grocery store as a checker and Jimmy was working full time with the doctor.

This year Jimmy's duties had expanded to include checking out the patients and getting them ready for the doctor. This meant wearing a white outfit like a medical professional. After getting their folders he would check their blood pressure, their heart rate, their weight, etc. He then asked them some basic questions, made notations in their folders and had them wait for the doctor. In addition he did odd jobs for the clinic.

For his work in the clinic he received the same pay as last year. Twenty a week spending money and funds to go back to school with when the time came.

Jimmy spent time with Mike whenever he could. They had been swimming several times and to the movies a few times. Mike liked to walk in the woods. They had done this on a several occasions. While out in the woods one day, they came by the entrance to the tunnel. It had pretty much grown back over. Jimmy decided to show it to him. They cleared their way to get inside. Jimmy was still able to make it over in the dark. He held Mike by the hand on the way over and assured him that it would be alright.

When they got to the other side they both took in the view. Jimmy felt a rush of emotions. He had thought he was completely over Carol but now he doubted if he ever would be. He could live with it but she would always be a part of him.

They had been walking for some time so they decided to stop there and take a rest. Jimmy looked around and found his old chest. He showed it to Mike. There were still paper and pencils in it. Mike took them out and sat down to rest. As he sat there he started to draw the valley below. At first Jimmy didn't notice but when he did, he couldn't believe his eyes. The drawing was really good and for a child his age it was outstanding. Jimmy didn't say anything until he was finished. Then he complimented him on it. He asked him how long he had been drawing?

"Not long. Homer didn't like me to draw. He said you were a sissy if you drew pictures."

Jimmy put one hand on each of his shoulders and said, "Mike, that's not true. As a matter of fact I would like to have that picture you just drew. May I have it?"

"Sure," said Mike handing him the picture.

They walked back to the dirt road and drove home.

That night Jimmy told Hilda and Bob about what happened at the tunnel. He showed them the picture he had been given. They all thought it was good and that Mike had a talent that needed to be explored.

While working in the clinic that summer Jimmy paid particular attention to how the doctor handled his patients. He knew them all by their first name. You could tell he had real affection for them. They, in turn, trusted him completely. That seemed to be a big part of the job. By the time he was ready to go back to school, Jimmy knew what kind of doctor he wanted to be.

The first thing Jimmy did when he got back to school was frame and hang the picture that Mike had given him. He liked Mike and he was glad he was with Bob and Hilda. He knew they would give him everything he needed.

Jimmy had decided to become a General Practitioner. He would not tell the department heads of his decision, yet, because he liked the attention he was getting from each of them. He knew how valuable that attention was to his learning.

One of last year's grads had left a set of weights and a bench when he departed. He had them moved to his room. The set of weights only went to one hundred and ten pounds so he purchased an additional one hundred pounds. He got a book on weight lifting from the library and started to work out early in the morning. His days now started with him rolling out of bed and working on the weights for an hour. Then he would clean up and be on his way.

After doing this for a month he noticed he was feeling better. Actually, he felt more alert. In addition his pants were fitting a little loose. He hadn't lost any weight, his body was just shaping up.

The formal posting as to where students would be going came out. As expected he would be coming back the following year. He was surprised that some of those he thought would be coming back weren't. As the year went on an occasional cheer could be heard when one of the students got notified that they were accepted somewhere for medical school.

It was almost the end of the year. Jimmy was called into the office. Since he had told them he wanted to be a General Practitioner things seemed to turn cold. Dr. Roberts and two of the department heads were in the office when he arrived. They asked if he still wanted to be a G.P? He said, "Yes." They paused for a minute, then one of the department heads asked Jimmy how much money he felt he could pay toward his future education there? He said the only money he had that could be applied to schooling was what he made at the library. They asked about his family. He said that his mother and father were divorced. His father had not had anything to do with the family in years. His mother had remarried a couple of years ago and he was all on his own.

Jimmy said he thought he was to continue on there on a scholarship. If that was not the case why did they let him think that? He could have had his application in at several other places. Now it was too late. They didn't say a word. They asked him to wait outside.

A few minutes later he was called back in. They didn't want him to be a G.P. If he went into a higher pro-file field he could, over the years, shed more recognition on the school. Before they could say another word he said, "I know a man who has been the father I never had. He went to medical school many years ago. Then he came to a small town that had no doctor. He is there today. He knows everyone in that town and is like a father to them all. They, in turn, love and respect him. He has been there for almost forty years and do you know he never had to mail out one bill? That's what I want to be someday. If I can not learn to be that here, then it will be somewhere else." He turned to leave and they stopped him.

Dr. Roberts said, "Jimmy, we want you to learn that here."

---

# *Chapter Twelve*

Next year, Jimmy would be moving into a new section of the college. He couldn't leave anything where he was because he wouldn't be coming back. He was given permission to store his weights in an unused closet at the library.

Bob and Hilda came up for his graduation. It was nothing special but it was nice to have them there. Dr. Rhodes was going to come but at the last minute he had to back out. He had a problem at the clinic.

With the car loaded there was just room for Jimmy to fit in himself. He was glad when he got home. As he unloaded his car he wondered why he had brought some of his stuff. He pitched several things without bringing them into the house. Mike was there waiting for him and he helped him unload and get squared away. Jimmy asked Mike if he would mind sharing his bedroom with him again this year. He just smiled.

After he got settled in, Mike could hardly wait to show him some drawings he had done. The bedroom was half full of his drawings. Jimmy was impressed. Mike must have been back to the tunnel because some of the pictures were valley views from there. When asked he said he hadn't been back, that he remembered it from before.

He told Jimmy that he would like to go back to the tunnel as he had liked it very much.

Jimmy noticed that several of the pictures were in color. He asked about them. Mike told him that there was a lady in town who was giving him lessons on the weekends. She had been a big help.

Bob was busy with someone in his office. Jimmy didn't get to talk to him until Hilda got home. They had news. Bobby was getting married that very next weekend in Pittsburgh. The whole family was going to the wedding. Dr. Rhodes had arranged to have his clinic covered and he was going, also. He had not attended Jimmy's graduation but he wasn't going to miss out this time. He was going. They planned to get there the day before and leave the day after the wedding. Bob had agreed to buy a new outfit for everyone. They would go shopping tomorrow to give everybody a chance to get what they wanted and time to have alterations made if necessary.

Jimmy asked Bob if that meant him, also. He said, "Bob, you know you really do not have to do that."

Bob said, "If you can't help those you love who can you help? However in your case, I will expect payment in full. That payment will be that you take Mike with you and see that he gets what he needs."

Jimmy thanked Bob and said that he was grateful that he and Hilda had found each other.

Jimmy was back working at the clinic. Dr. Rhodes's new car happened to be a van. It was easier for him to get in and out of. In addition he could carry more stuff and bring someone back to the clinic if he had to.

They decided to take the van on the trip to Pittsburgh. Jimmy was given the task of getting it ready. It was a full size van with four captain's seats and a bench that folded into a bed. The doctor had a habit of putting stuff in the van but he never took anything out. Jimmy asked Mike to help him unload it. Afterward, they cleaned the van inside and out, filled it with gas and loaded the luggage. With just room to spare for the passengers, they all piled in and were on the road. Jimmy was the driver. The doctor sat next to him. Directly behind them were Bob and Hilda. Kathy and Mike were on the bench.

Pittsburgh was only a few hours away. When they got there they checked into the hotel. They were assigned rooms on the tenth floor. Their windows faced the rivers. so they could look down and see where the Ohio river was formed. They could also see the ball field that they had seen so many times on television.

Shortly after they got to the hotel, Susan called. She had made arrangements for them to be picked up that evening. They would be going to dinner with her family and the wedding party after the wedding rehearsal. A limo would be picking them up at about eight p.m. None of them had ever been in a limo before. It was good that they each brought two good outfits. They started getting ready.

Soon the limo arrived and they were off to dinner.

The restaurant they went to was nice. There were about twenty people there in a private room. Everyone got a chance to meet and talk.

Susan's parents seemed like nice people.

Someone mentioned that the wedding must be very expensive. Susan's father said he didn't care what it cost. This was his baby girl. She was his one and only and if you were going to do something just once in your life, you might as well do it up right.

They did the wedding up just fine. Everything went like clock work. The reception was grand. Bobby was married in his uniform. His navy friends were there to salute them as well.

In the van on the ride home the next day the conversation was all about the wedding. No one would have changed a thing. It was perfect!

Jimmy had hoped to talk to Bobby more but there just wasn't time. He said that things were fine at school and it looked like it would take another two years. He also said he would have to give the navy some active time for all the time he spent in school. When he finished he would be almost half way to retirement age in the military. He wasn't sure what he would do at that point. He didn't have to make that decision for several years.

Back at home things settled into the usual summer routine. Kathy liked school and she looked forward to returning there in the fall. Jimmy was again working for the doctor. Mike had made the most change from last year. Aside from growing an inch or two, his whole personality had changed. He was no longer the shy quiet guy he was last year. He was happy, outgoing and full of life. Hilda had already started to work her magic on him.

One day late into the summer, things were slow at the clinic. Jimmy was working with some files when he came across a name that got his attention. It was Carol's file and there was another file inside it. He couldn't resist peeking. Carol had been to the doctor that past winter. She must have been home visiting her folks. She had brought a two year old boy with her to the doctor's. He had a fever and his name was Jimmy.

He put the folder down and went in to see the Dr. Rhodes. He mentioned the folder to him.

"Well, Jimmy, if you must know we have been putting that folder up each year before you got home for the summer. Apparently, we forgot this year. By the way, you must realize that this folder is none of your business."

The doctor felt bad after he said that.

Jimmy said, "I know its not. I just wondered how they were doing."

"Well, as you know she lives and works out of state. Where I don't know. She has been coming here each winter to see her folks. Once or twice she has come in here with a medical problem."

Jimmy said he thought she had given the child up but apparently she had not. "Is she alright, doctor?"

Dr. Rhodes took his glasses off and put them on the desk. "Do you know what you are asking? You know I cannot discuss things like that, but I can tell you this. She has asked about you every time she has been here and that's not part of the medical record."

Jimmy left the office and went back to his filing

work.

Jimmy went back to school a few days early. He would be staying in a new dorm and he wanted to get things set up before school started. He was back to his weight routine. He was surprised how much strength he had lost over the two months he hadn't used the weights.

After Jimmy had worked out with the weights for his second year he had achieved his goal. He was lifting four hundred twenty-five pounds. This was for the bench press and without a spotter. He stood six feet four and his weight was two hundred twenty pounds. With all the work he had done he still had to wear a shirt to cover the marks that Homer had given him. After all that time, his back was still hard to look at.

Jimmy's complexion was light. As he grew older his hair had darkened to almost black. His deep blue eyes sparkled when he smiled. He could have been distracted from his studies easily with the attention he received from women. For some reason he rarely paid attention to their advances nor did he initiate them himself.

The work load at school changed and he had to adjust to it a little. There were many new faces, kids that had come in from other schools. There were one hundred twenty students in the med school class. The learning groups were smaller. Jimmy's new roommate was from Chicago. He didn't seem like he would be needing much help from him like some of the others had.

Jimmy got engrossed in the work. It was the first time he really had to put out a major effort to maintain high grades. He didn't care though, he enjoyed the learning process.

Jimmy got the message that Homer was dead. It seems that he had been drinking. Apparently, he pulled his truck off the road and fell asleep. While he was asleep someone came up to his truck and put a bullet in his head. The police had no leads.

Jimmy thought about Homer. It had been twelve years since he and Hilda got their divorce. It didn't seem that long. In his mind, at times, he could still feel that belt on his back. The way that Homer was. The way he treated people. It seemed just a matter of time until someone put him in his place. However he felt sorry for Homer. Not only for what had happened to him and his family but for the life he had lived and all the pain he had caused.

It had been a few days since Hilda had heard about Homer being shot. He had been on her mind a few times. She wondered again what made him so mean. It couldn't have been something she had done because he had been that way from the beginning. Homer wasn't a big man but from the way he acted you would have thought he was a giant. He always seemed to piss everyone off and because of it his bell rang more than once. There was something about him that irritated people when they first laid eyes on him.

Homer was about five feet ten inches tall and he weighed around one hundred forty pounds. His brown hair was straight and hard to keep in place. The baseball cap he usually wore needed to be cleaned. His left eye did not open as well as the right one. When he was mad and about to blow up his left eye would twitch.

It was these and other things about Homer that were going through Hilda's mind when she got the phone call. It was from Mr. Kozel, the manager of the mine where he worked. He was calling her about Homer's insurance. He told Hilda that Homer had never taken her name off the insurance policy after they were divorced. There was also a matter of money he had paid into a retirement fund, plus vacation and present pay. In total it came to over thirty thousand dollars. Homer had no other living relatives that he was aware of, therefore, she would be getting the money in a few days.

Hilda put the phone down. She was in a daze. She had heard what Mr. Kozel had said but it had not sunk in. She went to Bob and told him what she had learned. As was his nature Bob took over.

He called the county to find out what had been done with Homer's body. It was still in the county morgue. A check was run on any outstanding debts, etc. To his credit Homer had lived the last few years of his life in a debt free status. He lived in a rented apartment and had a truck. Bob cleaned all these matters up and had enough money left over for a reasonable funeral expense.

Bob talked with Hilda about Homer's funeral expenses. She ran it over in her mind a few times and decided to have him cremated. She felt that if it was good enough for her grandfather it was good enough for Homer.

Hilda called the boys to see if they wanted to come

home. They, in turn, talked to each other. They wanted her to keep the ashes for them until the up coming summer and they would take care of them.

That summer when they were home they rode out to where the old house was in the hollow. They walked over to the bench where Hilda liked to sit. They poured the ashes into the creek. Bobby said it was fitting that his ashes be put into the acid creek. It was like he had been all his life, burning inside and slapping out at people. Jimmy said that he hoped that wherever Homer was the acid had been burned out of him and he could be a different person. Then they threw the urn in the creek after the ashes.

One of Jimmy's professors, Dr. Clark, had taken a special interest in him. They talked after class frequently. He had invited Jimmy over to his home for dinner several times. He was an interesting man and he had been helpful with Jimmy's studies. Jimmy was very fond of him. It was good to have someone to go to when you had something on your mind.

On one of his visits Dr. Clark told Jimmy this story. There was a very wealthy man by the name of Thompson who lived in Pittsburgh. A few years back he came to school and asked them if they had any projects that needed funding. At the time, they wanted to build a new wing on the hospital. He asked how much it would cost? He was told about ten million. He said fine. He would give them one million dollars for every year they could keep him alive. If they kept him alive for ten years they would have their wing. This sounded like a good deal. They checked him out thoroughly and found a few problems. None were life or death matters. With reasonable care he should live out the ten years. It was agreed that he would follow all instructions given by the doctors. A live in nurse was assigned to see that he followed their instructions and to monitor his general condition. Everything went well for six years when he died rather unexpectedly. Jimmy thought. What rich people won't think of.

Jimmy had spent four years at college. Aside from students, he had made friends on staff as well. When he was leaving it was as if he was leaving home to go home.

When he arrived Mike was on the porch waiting for him. Jimmy had been his summer buddy now for a couple years. Kathy was at home and she was liking it more than the school she was going to. Hilda told them that Bobby wouldn't be coming this summer. Susan was expecting and with his school load they couldn't get away.

Jimmy suggested that they take a pay Bobby a visit. That was shot down but that night after dinner, they all made up a list of things for the baby. They would all pitch in and buy them. This was done over the next week. They boxed everything up and shipped it. They put a note with it that said they had a local baby shower and this was the result. There were eight boxes of stuff. Even the doctor and the people from the grocery store put items in. The baby was due to arrive just before they would be going back to school.

Jimmy was working in the Doctor's office again.

Things were the same there. The doctor was looking his age but he was still going strong.

Jimmy kept being pulled to the files. One day when he felt it was safe, he looked at Carol's file. They had been in again that winter. This was one hell of a way to keep in touch with an old friend. He put the file back and told himself that it would be the last time he looked at it.

For the first time Jimmy took a hard look at Franklin and the area around it. As the mines closed, one after the other, the population grew smaller. The mines produced more coal with fewer people. There were fewer of them, also. For home use people were converting to gas and this hit the small coal mines. There was still farming and a few light industries, like a shirt factory.

The big change was in the people. Some young people were leaving in order to find a better opportunity for a life. They had lost almost a whole generation for the lack of having opportunity, locally. For the most part the people who were left were older. They either had enough time in not to be laid off, or they had enough time in to retire when the mine closed. The average age was several years above the national average. It was a shame that the people who had opened and run the mines had raped the area. Valleys that once were fertile were now barren. Their streams and creeks were unable to support life because of the red acid mine run off. Where the mines were not bleeding into streams, the earth was scared with ugly marks of strip mines.

All the fish and wildlife that these streams once supported were gone. Many felt that the area would have been better off if it never had coal. If some good jobs weren't found in the area Franklin like the hollow would die. It was just a matter of time.

The next door neighbor had a niece come to spend the summer. Her name was Pat. She had finished high school and would be starting college. She was tall, good looking and she had an eye on Jimmy. One day Mike and Jimmy ran into her while swimming. In a bathing outfit she was a knock out. All heads turned her way when she walked by. She spent most of the afternoon with them. Jimmy finally took her out on a date. After that they went out a few more times but they didn't hit it off. It was Jimmy's first time out with a girl who had been around the block a few times and liked it. She wanted more from him than he was willing to give, so to speak. He managed to get away unmarked.

In late August there was a fire in one of the mines. They called for the doctor. Some men were trapped in the mines. There were two men who had been burned badly. The doctor asked Jimmy to come along. They got into the van and drove a few miles to the mine. It was the one where Homer had worked. When they got there they saw the two burn victims. They were in real bad shape. They called to have them air lifted to a regional hospital. The doctor could do little for them but make them more comfortable. Large pieces of skin on their exposed arms looked like it was just melting off.

There were two or three others still trapped in the mine. The doctor didn't think his waiting there would help them any. With the amount of smoke coming out of the mine he felt there was little chance they would make it. Later he proved to be right.

As they drove back to the clinic Jimmy couldn't get those men out of his mind. It was the amount of pain they were in that got to him.

As Jimmy drove back to school he realized that this would be his last full summer at home. They had told him that he needed to spend his next summer at college. After Med school he would have to spend eighteen months at a hospital. Then he would be done. That added up to three and a half more years.

---

# *Chapter Thirteen*

One of Jimmy's concerns was that he might get tired of going to school. He was starting his seventeenth year. So far he still looked forward to the challenge. With the new students coming in from other schools last year he was afraid that he wouldn't be able to keep his number one ranking. He was right. He fell to second place last year. He was determined to correct that placement this year. He believed he had the ability and he owed it to his future patients to do his very best.

With the work load, both from school and that which he put on himself, there was little time for a social life. There were several girls in the med school. They were working as hard as he with the same social impact.

Jimmy and his new roommate, Mark, decided to ask two girls from the class to form a study group. It was just that, a study group. They began to share other chores. They would take turns cooking, taking wash to the laundry and several other things. The net effect was that it freed up a little time for each of them. The group was to stay together for the remainder of time they were there.

This year Dr. Rhodes had given Jimmy an increase in pay for his work at the clinic. With more income he decided to give up his job at the library. After a couple weeks they asked him to come back. They had received several requests from students he had been helping for him to return. They agreed to give him a pay raise.

The work load at school just melted into a routine and time passed. Once in a while he would hear from home. Everything there was alright.

He couldn't look forward to spending the summer at home. For his birthday, before school started again in the fall, the family came to pay him a visit. He had not realized how much he missed them until they came. He was so glad to see them. Mike was becoming a young man. They told him that Bobby had received his doctorate degree. He would be stationed in Connecticut and working on submarines. They said he had been promoted to Lieutenant Commander.

The family stayed overnight and went back home. Kathy was looking forward to her last year in school. After her training she was going to work for Dr. Rhodes. Before Bob left, he gave Jimmy some money. He said that he and Dr. Rhodes knew he would be needing it and had both contributed equally. It was the same amount as if he had worked the summer. He thanked him and said he hoped it would be the last time he needed it. After this year when he started his internship he would receive some pay. Not much, but he hoped he could get along on it.

The fall term started again. This would be his last. The study group fired up as they had last year. This year there was alot of talk about where people were going to spend their internships, and where those who were going to specialize would be going to get extra training.

That topic seemed to be as on going as the studies themselves. Dr. Roberts had already informed Jimmy that he could stay on at the hospital there. After thinking it over and without telling him Jimmy had applied and had been accepted at Cook County General in Chicago. The hospital at the college was a good one. On the down side, it was small and in a remote area. You would get a bigger variety of cases at Cook County General in one month than you would get here in a year. Besides that it was time for a change.

After he had been accepted in Chicago, he told Dr. Roberts. He accepted Jimmy's decision and wished him well.

There wasn't much fuss made at graduation. Most of the students just said their goodbyes when they were finished taking their exams. Then they cleared out and went home. That's what Jimmy did. When he loaded the car and pulled away for the last time his mind wandered. He thought back to the day he had arrived. He had finished more than eight years of schooling in seven years. He had a degree in medicine. He had earned the title of Doctor. He couldn't practice until after his eighteen months in Chicago but by God, he was a Doctor.

It didn't seem possible that eight years had gone by. He looked back to that boy who arrived there and how he felt then and now and he knew it had been every bit of seven years.

Jimmy would have only three weeks at home before leaving for Chicago. He talked to Bob and he thought he might want to look for another car. The bug he had was eight years old. It still ran good but maybe it should go.

After talking to Dr. Rhodes at the clinic the next day, he decided to keep it and see if it would last another eighteen months. What they didn't tell you when you applied to the hospital was about the area around it. He would be less likely to have problems with an old car.

During the time Jimmy was home that summer he spent some time at the clinic. He couldn't keep himself from looking at Carol's file. She had not been back in the last two years.

After looking at the records he began to think about what he wanted to do with the rest of his life. He had been so busy these past several years that not having a woman in his life seemed natural. There was no time. If Carol had waited they probably would be getting married about now. He knew he loved children. He had no way of predicting his future. Only time would tell.

Mike had made some friends and he spent most of the summer doing what fifteen year olds do. He and Jimmy spent little time together. Jimmy had a chance to check out his artwork. It was growing up at about the same rate he was. There were some drawings and a few paintings of nude women. Jimmy asked him about them and where he got his models? He said that when he went swimming he just pictured the girls  without their bathing suits on.

Mike was almost six feet tall. He was almost all

arms and legs. He had not started to fill out yet. He had noticed that unlike him and his other brothers at that age, Mike didn't have a job. He mentioned this to Bob. He simply said that they were fortunate to be in a position that unlike when he was his age, they didn't need help with the money. Further, he said that Mike, like most people, would be working most of his life. A little time now to enjoy growing up, after what he had been through when he was young, might just help balance things out.

Jimmy said he wasn't suggesting that Mike have to work. He felt that working when he was young helped him. He hadn't realized that in some cases his working got him away from a bigger problem. A problem that Mike didn't have at this time. Besides, his drawing and his painting were like studying for him.

The car made it to Chicago. Now he only had eighteen months to go. The doctor was right. The car fit into this area well. For whatever reason, possibly pity or sorrow for the owner, the car was never bothered with the entire time he was there.

Jimmy had to get adjusted to the area. The city driving was unreal. At times, he wished he was driving a tank instead of that bug.

He had asked that someone from the hospital find him a place to stay. The told him about a place where most of the new interns stayed. The rental price seemed high but manageable so he took it. His living quarters weren't far from his work. He thought about buying a bike. One of his fellow interns said he had one for all of two weeks before it was stolen. He thought of walking but that turned out to be a bad idea as well.

Jimmy was meeting a number of of new people. They all seemed to get along well. Maybe that was because they had a common goal. The hours were long, too long. It seemed that he was always either working or sleeping. He felt more than once that this was as much an endurance test as a learning process.

Jimmy got a little piece of luck after he was there a few months. A man was brought in who had been in a car accident. He ended up in Jimmy's ward. They started talking. The man was about forty-five years old. He was born and was raised in Franklin. His family had moved away when he was fifteen. His father had lost his job in the mines and they had to move. He was in the life insurance business. They needed someone to go to people's houses and give them physicals whenever they bought a policy. He asked Jimmy if he would be interested in the position? He knew he was working long hours but he knew, also, how little they paid interns. One advantage was that Jimmy could make his appointments with the people when it fit into his schedule. He could work as little or as much as he wanted. He accepted the position, thus putting an end to his cash flow problems while in Chicago.

After about six months Jimmy got a two week break. At first, he had only driven the few blocks to and from the hospital. Now he was driving all over town. He thought about buying a better car. Instead of going home, he decided to do as many physicals as possible so he set up as many appointments as he could. With the help of his friend from Franklin he was doing eight or ten a day. After ten days he had made almost five thousand dollars. Looking at the balance in his check book, he liked what he saw. He decided to keep his car.

His original assessment of the amount and variety of work at the hospital was an understatement. On weekend. the patient traffic was unreal. With the shootings and stabbings alone, he felt like he was in a war zone. He was glad he had made the decision to come there but he would be relieved when it was over. How some people could tear each other apart the way they did, he just couldn't understand.

Dr. Rhodes called Jimmy at his apartment. He asked him how he was doing and about things in general. Jimmy sensed that he had something on his mind and hoped it wasn't that someone was in trouble. Finally, the doctor got to the point of his call. He wanted to know if Jimmy could like to come and work with him in his clinic. He was having trouble keeping up with the work load. If Jimmy would join him he could cut his schedule in half. Then in a few years the clinic would be his when he retired.

Jimmy said, "Yes." He had been looking for a way to approach Dr. Rhodes about just this thing. He had always wanted to be at the clinic. He thanked him very much for the offer and told him he would be there in a few months.

When Jimmy hung up the phone it was as if a great

weight had been lifted off his back. He would be finished at the hospital in three months. He felt like there was a wall at the end of that time frame. That was because he hadn't made arrangements for anything beyond that point. He felt so good that he wished he had asked the doctor about this long ago.

With the money he had saved from his insurance appointments, he decided to buy a new Ford four door sedan. After his last duties at the hospital he loaded the bug and headed to the Ford dealer where he traded it in. He unloaded the bug and loaded the Ford. He was on the road by ten a.m.

Driving that new car made him feel like a big shot. There were just a few times in his life when he had driven a car that he didn't have to say a prayer that he would make it.

He didn't mind leaving the hospital behind. He had learned alot there but it was a rough place. He wondered how people could spend their lives working there. It would take a stronger person than he was.

As Jimmy drove into Franklin it felt different this time. He was home and that was good. Knowing that he didn't have to leave again made the difference.

———————————

# *Chapter Fourteen*

When Jimmy got to the house everyone seemed to be keeping themselves at a distance. He couldn't put his finger on it but something must have been wrong. He unpacked and moved into the room with Mike.

Hilda said she had made plans for the family to go out to dinner. There was only one real nice restaurant in town and they would be going there. She asked Jimmy if he needed to have anything cleaned or pressed to go out with them. He said no.

It was early spring. The leaves had not started to show yet. Jimmy decided to use what was left of the afternoon to look for an apartment. There wasn't much available. It didn't take long to cover most of the town. The few apartments that were there were full. That left three houses to select from. He chose the smallest of the group and put down a deposit. The house was just two blocks from the clinic. On nice days he could walk.

While in the area he stopped in to see the doctor. He was quite busy so Jimmy just let him know that he was in town. After assessing the situation at the clinic Jimmy thought his plan to take a few weeks off might not have been such a good one. With his age and work load the doctor needed help. He decided to cut his time off to one week. This would give him time to get moved into his new place and get things set up.

That evening while everyone was getting ready for dinner Jimmy told them about his renting the house. Hilda asked him what he was going to use for furniture? He said he would buy what he could afford and live with it until he could do better.

Bob had heard the conversation. He said that one of the reasons he built such a large garage when they first improved the house was to store some of the furniture from his first marriage. They could look at that and Jimmy was welcome to have anything he thought he could use.

They left for the restaurant. When they arrived the parking lot was packed. Jimmy never remembered it being this busy. When he went in he knew why. It was a surprise party for him. Almost the whole town was there. They had taken over the entire restaurant. He was surprised! They had a band there and there was dancing. The dinner was great and there were toasts. When one of those giving a toast mentioned that Jimmy was the first person from Franklin to become a doctor, Hilda said no. She stood up and said he was the second. Her son, Bobby, who had arrived late for the party, was the first. Jimmy was the first medical doctor.

All in all it was a great night. Seeing Bobby again was really swell. It was the first time Jimmy had seen him in a regular suit and not in his navy outfit.

Susan looked wonderful! They now had a boy and a girl and were thinking about one more to round out their family.

Bobby was a full commander. He was stationed at the submarine base. He said it was odd but he hadn't been out to sea since since he had joined the navy. He had been in the navy for ten years. Jimmy asked him what his plans were? Didn't he think he could make more money outside the navy with his education? He said he probably could but that the navy had given him that same education. He would be making captain shortly and he liked what he was doing. Most of which he couldn't talk about. He had decided to make a career in the navy.

Kathy had been working in the clinic for more than a year. As Jimmy was to find out she just about ran the place. She had told the family several times that she didn't think the work at the clinic was what she wanted to do. However she didn't have an idea about what she would like to do.

The party was over. They were driving back to the house. What Kathy had said bothered Jimmy. When the others had gone to bed they sat at the kitchen table and talked. She said everything at the clinic was fine. She liked the doctor and the people but she didn't feel she was doing was enough for herself. He asked Kathy if she had discussed this with the doctor. She said she had. She had told him when Jimmy got there and was settled in, she would be leaving.

Kathy was on Jimmy's mind the entire week. As he went about setting up the house he wondered what was bothering her. He knew she loved medicine. While he went through the Bob's furniture and shopped, a plan was forming. He was overwhelmed at what it cost just to buy the things he needed for the kitchen. His bank balance, what there was left of it, had crashed. Without help from the garage he couldn't have made it.

Jimmy called the school where Kathy had gone. He acted like a doctor to whom she had applied for work. He asked for a copy of her records. Upon reviewing them, he he saw that she had been an outstanding student. He was not surprised. On more than one occasion, some of her professors had made a statement that they thought she should have gone on to medical school.

On his first day at work in the clinic, Jimmy shared the information with the Dr. Rhodes. They called Kathy in after work and discussed her problem. They told her they felt her problem was that underneath, she wanted to be a doctor. That working as a nurse just frustrated her.

They called Bob and Hilda and invited themselves for dinner that night. At dinner they discussed what they had gone over with Kathy in the clinic. Kathy admitted that she had always wanted to be a doctor. She said she felt better now that it was out on the table.

"That's all good Kathy," Jimmy said, "but you have just wasted the better part of three years working at the clinic."

She said she didn't think working at the clinic had been a waste of time. Jimmy felt stupid for even saying it.

The big question was asked. Do you want to go to medical school now?

"'Yes, yes," she said.

"Well, how do we go about making that happen Dr. Rhodes?" Bob asked. We'll just have to work it out was his answer.

It was early March. They still had an outside chance of getting her into a school this fall. Dr. Rhodes and Jimmy would work on it.

Then there was the matter of money. It could cost quite a bit. They didn't think she would qualify for a scholarship. It was agreed upon that if Kathy could get into a school that the cost would be split four ways. Hilda, who had said she was going to quit working, said that she would continue. Bob, Jimmy and the doctor agreed to take on a share.

Kathy had worked for almost three years. She had stayed at home and had saved quite a bit on her own. In addition, she had a one year old car that was paid for.

Dr. Rhodes and Jimmy made several phone calls and put out feeders. Some of the places they thought might come through were already full for the fall term.

About two weeks later Jimmy got a phone call from Dr. Clark, his teacher and friend from medical school. He had accepted a position at a state run college. They still had a couple of openings. He said he would be glad to hold one of them open pending his review of Kathy's records.

They assembled Kathy's records along with several recommendations from nursing school. Both Dr. Rhodes and Jimmy wrote recommendations with high praise. They hoped it would be enough. Because of getting a late start on applying, Dr. Clark said when she was ready she could call for an appointment, bring her records and visit the school.

Kathy was ready. The appointment was made. The last few days before she left for the school, she was a nervous wreck. Jimmy felt that if she didn't leave soon she would explode.

When she got to the school she met with Dr. Clark. As Jimmy had said he was a very nice individual. While she was in his office he asked her several questions. One of which was why she hadn't started to medical school sooner? She said she couldn't. That it was all the family could do to support one and Jimmy was already in school. She didn't feel she had a right to ask. Several other questions were asked and answered. In less than an hour she was on her way home. He said she would be notified in about a week to ten days if she was accepted.

On her drive home she went over everything that happened in that office. She hoped she had made a good impression but it was hard to tell. She felt she had properly answered all of his questions. She said a few prayers and left it in God's hands.

Back home that night she had trouble sleeping. That was rare for her as she usually slept like a log. As the days passed and got close to the ten day time frame, she was beside herself. Kathy was pure hell to be around. The tenth day went by and nothing. She asked Jimmy to call but he refused. On the twelfth day it arrived. She went home for lunch to check the mail and it was there. She brought the letter back to the office with her heart literally pounding out of her chest. She handed it to her mother to open. As Hilda started to open the letter Kathy stepped back and put her hands up to her face. It looked like she was prepared to hold in a cry if it was bad news. Hilda started to read the letter out loud. She read to line five before she got to the part that said she was accepted. They both cheered to the top of their voices. A clinic wasn't the best place to do that. Both doctors came in to see what was going on. They too cheered and did a little dance around the reception area. The patients who were seated there must have thought they had gone out of their minds.

For as low as Kathy had been in the recent past, now she was high. She seemed like a new person and she was. She was going to live her lifetime dream, she was going to be a doctor.

One day there was a slow period at the office. Jimmy sat at his desk and had some time to think. He was now twenty-seven years old and just starting his life as a doctor. Kathy was twenty-five and just starting medical school. That and being an intern would keep her busy for five or six years. Bobby was now a Captain. He and Susan were expecting their third child. Bobby was twenty-nine. Jimmy had talked to a retired service man and he said that being a Captain at that age was quite an accomplishment. Bobby was still going to stay in the navy.

Mike was seventeen and almost as big as Jimmy. He was starting his last year of high school. He was still very interested in art. He had become very good at it. The local lady who had been teaching him said she had taught him all she could. He was talking about going to an art school after high school. Bob thought he should go to a regular college and after that if he still wanted to go to an art school, fine.

Mike had developed a good sense of humor. He also had been drawing a cartoon character that he named Big Zero. Big Zero was just what his name suggested. He was a big individual with a rounded body who was dumb. He drew jokes in which Big Zero was doing something stupid. The local newspaper had printed a few of them and they had been received very well. A few other papers wanted to pick them up. Mike was now making nearly two hundred dollars per drawing. Hilda and Bob were mighty proud of him.

The Welch's were beginning their tenth year of marriage. If you didn't know their past you would have thought they had been married all of their lives. Bob had fit into their family well. He was a good man. Jimmy often wondered how his life would have been if Bob had been his real father. From time to time he still thought of Homer. When he did he tried to get him out of his mind as fast as he could.

Franklin had lost some population. The county as a whole had not. It had become a well kept secret that some of the retired folks from the big eastern cities had moved there because of the lower cost of living. Some of them liked the open spaces. Some had been born and raised there and were just coming back home.

This had an impact on the clinic. With the same but older population it meant more work. On the average older folks needed more medical attention than the young. In addition over the years a doctor or two, who had been on the fringe of the clinic trade area, had retired or moved on and had not been replaced. The net effect on the clinic was that in the near future it would have to be enlarged. It would not be many years before it would need two full time doctors.

Jimmy had taken a hard look at Dr. Rhodes. He needed to slow down. As they discussed, in a couple of months, he would cut his work load in half. Jimmy felt comfortable with that arrangement. He wondered how long the doctor would want to work at that reduced rate. He hoped he wouldn't have to carry the full load himself. Dr. Rhodes was now sixty-eight years old. He was fit and in pretty good shape for that age. Jimmy wondered how long he would have him.

It was time for Kathy to be off to school. She was really looking forward to it. Jimmy wondered if she had any idea of how hard she was going to buckle down the next several years. Whatever she needed to do he was sure she would do it.

---

# *Chapter Fifteen*

The work at the clinic was going along just fine. Dr. Rhodes was working there three days a week. Every time you saw him he always had a book in his hand. He had started going fishing again.

One Sunday he invited Jimmy to go on one of his fishing trips. They drove a few miles from town and up into the mountains. They stopped at a farmer's house. They were on his property. There was a small stream that ran for about two miles on his farm. It had several ponds on it that looked man made.

Jimmy recognized the farmer as one of his patients from the clinic. Dr. Rhodes introduced him and they shook hands. He invited them into his house for a cup of coffee. Over coffee, Jimmy heard a story that he was sure Dr. Rhodes had listened to a few times before. The farmer, Mr. Freeman, went on to say that this farm had been in his family for five generations. Each generation had improved on it. His father had cleared the land by the creek and made the ponds. One of the things he had done was stock them with fish. He had two grown sons who had left the area and had no interest in farming. He was the last of his family who would be on the land.

The farm consisted of over two thousand acres. It was a dairy farm with fields for corn and hay as well as several pastures. Jimmy found out that this was the same creek that ran through the hollow where he had been raised. The farm was above the mines and up stream from all the bad run off. The area was beautiful. This must have been how it was all the way down to Franklin before the coal mines had dumped their mess into it.

Mr. Freeman mentioned as he had to Dr. Rhodes before, that there was only one rule for his guests who fished his stream and ponds. If you weren't going to eat the fish that day, you had to put it back.

That simple rule and the limited number of guests had kept the fishing plentiful for years. This day proved no exception. They each kept three fish. That night they had dinner with Hilda and Bob. The fish melted in your mouth. Jimmy had a great day. He was looking forward to going fishing with the doctor again. For a few days he kept thinking about how nice that farm had been.

Christmas had come and gone. It was good to see Kathy. It was also nice to hear she liked what she was doing and was doing it well. She wasn't number one in the class but she was in the top ten percent. Secretly, Jimmy was surprised that she was doing that well. She had been out of school for three years but obviously she had not gotten rusty.

Bobby alternated Christmases between Susan's family and his. This year was her family's turn.

In mid January Jimmy was at the clinic. He went out to say something to Hilda in the reception area. As he entered the room he saw Carol sitting there with her son.

The boy was nine years old. Seeing Carol, he forgot what he had come to tell Hilda. He went straight over to Carol. She stood up and they shook hands. Finally he said, "Carol, it's sure great to see you. Is everything alright?"

She said that before she had left to drive home her son had cut his arm in a fall. It wasn't serious but he had stitches that needed to be taken out. She asked where Dr. Rhodes was? He told her it was his day off but he would take care of the boy.

Carol was the last person he had to see that day. When she brought the boy in they had a little time to chat. She had heard he was going to be a doctor but thought he would move away from the area. He asked her how long she was going to be in town? She said for quite some time. Her mother had died the month before. Jimmy, almost forgetting, said he was sorry to hear that. She had a younger brother, fourteen years old. Since she had never married her father had asked her to come home and take care of the house for him and her brother.

She asked about him. He told her he had finished school and training, last year, and he had been working in the clinic since then. She asked if he was married. He said that so far he had not had the time. As she was leaving he mustered the courage to ask her out to dinner. He was happy when she accepted.

Carol had looked good when they were in high school. Now, several years later, she looked even better. She was five feet nine inches tall and about one hundred thirty pounds. She had changed her hair style but her face didn't look a day older. She had grown some in the bust area. This made her waist look smaller. Carol surely was easy to look at. Like Jimmy, she had not encouraged any man's advances. She said she had been content with her single status.

It was Friday night about seven when he pulled up to her door. She was sitting on the front porch waiting. She got in the car and they drove off. He asked about the whereabouts of her son and father. She said she had fixed them dinner and they had just sat down to eat. Jimmy thought he saw someone at one of the windows as they pulled away.

Carol sat as far away from him as she could. When they had been dating she would have been right on his shoulder. Dinner was just as formal. After dinner as they were having a cup of coffee Jimmy said, " Carol, what did I do wrong?"

"Wrong, my God Jimmy, you did nothing wrong. I have prayed to God just to be able to see you someday and to be able to ask you to forgive me." Tears were running down her face. She said she had no good excuse for what happened. She shouldn't have been dating much less having sex with a man. She had gone out with the boy a few times and they had sex only once. After she did it she felt sick. Sick for what she had done to him. Sick for what she had done to herself and the family. She had decided to write him a letter to tell him what happened. She was going to tell him that she was breaking up with him, that she didn't deserve him.

That was before she found out she was pregnant. When she found that out she felt her life had come to an end. What could she tell him that wouldn't hurt him more? She left town to live with her mother's younger sister. She was a school teacher and had no children. They planned to stay with her until the baby came. Then the baby would be put up for adoption.

Jimmy asked her why she didn't marry the man who had fathered her child. She said that had never been an option as far as she was concerned. She didn't love him. She saw him as another Homer.

Carol said her pregnancy had not been easy. With many trips to the doctor she was able to come to term. As when she was carrying the baby, the birth was a hard one. She had been operated on after the birth and was in the hospital for three weeks.

They told her that she could never have anymore children. She had been having a hard time with the fact that she was planning to give the baby away. This news put an end to that. How could she give her only child away? Her doctor explained the problem. He said there were several things wrong. He told her if she had not had that baby then she probably never could have had one. He said that the operation they performed would have been necessary in a year or so, anyway. Ever since then she felt lucky to have had her son, Jimmy.

He asked why she had called him Jimmy? She said, "You know why. You were the father I had always wished he had."

He asked Carol why she had never answered his letters? She said at the time she felt anything she could say to him would only hurt him more. When she had the baby and found out that she couldn't have anymore children, she thought she would be better off with someone else. She knew how much he loved children.

They finished their coffee and drove home. It was quiet in the car all the way. They both had alot to think about. When they got to her house he walked her to the door and said, "Would you please do me a favor? Let's pretend that we are at the tunnel and we are kissing good night." They took a long, soft kiss. She turned to the door and said, "Thank you, Jimmy," and went into the house.

During the next couple of weeks Jimmy was very busy, but still, he couldn't get Carol out of his mind. The night they had gone out she had been very formal. He wondered why she had gone with him. Maybe she just wanted a chance to explain. Then there was that good night kiss. There seemed to be feelings between them or was that just like the kiss he asked for. The kind of kissing they used to do.

He was thinking about how she looked. She had not put on any weight. She never was a fancy dresser but she looked good that night. There was one thing he knew. He wanted to see her again.

He was at home when he decided to call. Her father answered the phone. He said that she was taking a shower. Jimmy gave him his number and asked him if he would have her call him back. He had finished his dinner and was watching TV. After she didn't call him right back he fell asleep in the chair. He was awakened later by the phone. It was Carol. She said that her father had written her a note and gone to bed. She had just found it and hoped it wasn't too late to call.

Jimmy was so glad she called it was hard for him to begin talking. They carried on a conversation for awhile, mostly about nothing. Finally he said, "The reason I called is because I have been thinking alot about you. I have come to the conclusion that I want to see more of you. I want to see you often. Is that a problem?"

"No. As a matter of fact I came to that conclusion some time ago. I have been waiting for your call. What took you so long?"

"Well, you could say that I am a slow learner but you wouldn't believe it. I guess I was just afraid you might say, no."

They went out to dinner again the next night which was Saturday. Being together was great! They talked and talked. They sat at their table until it was almost closing time. When he dropped her off this time the kiss didn't have to be asked for. It came from both their hearts.

They decided to spend time together the next day. Carol said she would come by after church. She was there at nine A.M. When she rang the door bell he was just starting to cook breakfast, He teased that some of the neighbors might think she had spent the night there, She said she had quit worrying about what the neighbors were thinking a long time ago.

She had been up early and they had gone to early mass. She wanted to get an early start. He held her and they kissed again. This time they didn't want to part. Jimmy said, "For now, I think it is best that we keep our old agreement." She agreed.

By the end of the day they both knew they were in love again. In that short time he knew what he had been missing in his life. He also knew she was the missing part. She had never stopped loving him and she had not been with another man since she had her baby.

Jimmy asked her to marry him. She said, "Yes!" They talked about everything, including about how he might feel about her not being able to have his baby. He said that didn't matter. He felt that who raised the child was more important than who made the baby. He asked how she felt about him adopting Jimmy? She said she hoped he would and she loved him all the more for asking.

Things were going very fast. Jimmy wanted to set the date. She said the sooner the better.

"No," he said, "let's do it up right. We have waited all these years, we deserve a nice wedding. Shouldn't we get married in the church?"

"Sure, but you aren't Catholic."

"Well, I've always lived like one. I believe in God. I have read the Bible a few times and I live by the ten commandments. I will become Catholic. What will that take?"

They met the next day after the clinic closed. They

went to see the priest who was expecting them. They told him what they had in mind. He said he would give Jimmy instructions. After he was a member of the faith they could announce the bonds of marriage. He felt they could plan their marriage any time after three months. While they were there they selected a date and set up a time for Jimmy to get his instructions.

After leaving the church they went by and told Hilda and Bob. They were so glad for them. Hilda knew how much Jimmy loved Carol and thought, at times, that because of that he would never get married.

Then Jimmy drove Carol home. She invited him in. It was the first time he had been in that house since he was in high school. They told her father and brother. Her father shook Jimmy's hand. He said, "Thank God you two finally got together." He insisted on having a drink to toast the occasion. Jimmy didn't drink but this could be an exception. After the toast her father said he wished her mother had lived to see it. She had always liked Jimmy so much.

Jimmy wanted to see and tell Jimmy, Jr., but he was asleep.

He kissed Carol and headed home. Something her father said kept going around in his head. If only her mother had lived to see it. Maybe if she had lived Carol would not have come home. Sometimes things just don't add up.

The preparations for the wedding started to take on a life of their own. Jimmy had one more instruction to go before becoming a Catholic. His last concern was behind him now. He had been worried about how Carol's son, Jimmy, would take to him. He met the boy and they hit it off just grand. He already loved the boy but he felt more like a brother than a father. Maybe that would come with time.

With his last instruction class behind him Jimmy was about to become a Catholic. The day after he was baptized he was to have his first confession. Jimmy had given that a great deal of thought. He really wasn't looking forward to it. He went into the confessional and he started. When he got to the part where he began listing his sins he stopped. There was silence for awhile. Realizing that this was his first time the priest just said, "Go on." Jimmy said he wasn't sure what he should say. He said he always believed in God, and only one God. He didn't go to church on Sunday but that was before he was a Catholic. He had gone over the Ten Commandments and felt he was in pretty good shape. Since the doctor had given him that Bible when he was fifteen he had really tried to live by it. The priest said, "What about sex?"

He said he had only loved one woman in his life and that he had never had sex. He said, "Did you desire other people's things?"

"No," Jimmy said. He desired things but things he was willing to work for and get himself. Jimmy said, "Using the Ten Commandments is one thing that I have done."

"Did you honor your father and mother?" Then, Jimmy told the priest about Homer. Jimmy got the priest's blessing and left.

Carol's father insisted on paying for the wedding. It was a grand event. Carol looked quite outstanding in her wedding dress. Her father said it was wonderful to see her smiling again. Bobby and Kathy took time off to come. Bobby, Susan and the three children could have been put on a poster ad for the ideal looking family.

The wedding was on a Saturday. They drove to Niagara Falls where they spent almost a week. As they got to know each other they realized how much they had lost over the past nine years.

On their way home Carol sat so close to Jimmy that he thought he might have a problem driving but he liked it. Carol wanted to stop by and see the aunt who had helped her when she had her baby. They also had a favor to ask. Jimmy was introduced to Carol's aunt Ann. She said she had always wanted to meet Jimmy. She had heard so much about him. The favor they were asking for was a big one.

Ann knew Carol couldn't have anymore children. The favor they wanted was for her to help another young girl who was expecting. Then the girl would let Jimmy and Carol have her baby.

Ann said that she would have to think about it. She was planning on taking an early retirement from her teaching job. She said she wasn't as young as she used to be but she would let them know.

Just a few days before the wedding a young girl and her father came to the clinic. They found out she was expecting. They were poor farmers. Their religion ruled out aborting the baby. The father said if she kept the baby she wouldn't be able to finish school. At her age her life would be ruined and what chance would the baby have?

Jimmy told them to give him a few weeks to see if he could work something out.

When Carol and Jimmy arrived home there was a message waiting for them. Ann had called and said she would do it. She said, however, that she expected them to cover her expense.

Carol and Jimmy devised a plan. In the third or fourth month the girl would go and live with Ann. After delivery she would be told that the baby was given up for adoption. Ann, with some help, would keep the baby for a few months. Then Jimmy and Carol, it's adoptive parents, would bring it home. The time delay would serve to allow others not to think it was the local girl's baby. This might avoid future problems with her family.

Carol joked and said she was going to be in trouble again. She would be having a baby in less than nine months after she was married.

After all the commitments were made there was a potential problem. The girl was having twins. Carol and Jimmy were glad to hear the news but what did that do to their plans? They decided to bring one baby home after two months and the other after three months. They hoped people would think they were from two separate mothers. They also hoped they weren't identical twins.

Jimmy and young Jimmy bonded right from the

start. He was already calling him Dad. Carol started getting things together for the twins. They would have to get someone to help Ann for three months while she would be keeping them. Carol was making a list of things Ann would need as well as what she would need when she got the babies.

Carol shared their baby plans with her father. She could trust him to keep a secret. She was surprised when he said he would like to buy the initial items for the babies. He said she could keep them at his house until she needed them. That would be a big help.

Everything went according to plan. The babies were born in good health. They weren't identical. The babies had been with Ann for two months. The first baby was home now. Her father would be picking the second one up in four weeks. Aunt Ann said she would come back with him. She would stay a few days until Carol got the feel of things with the babies.

They were a boy and a girl. Jimmy and Carol had been married for less than a year. They had two boys and a girl. Their family was complete.

Since they were brought home so close together they said they would celebrate their birthdays on the same day.

There was so much love between Carol and Jimmy that it wrapped around the children as well.

The clinic was running like a top. Jimmy and Dr. Rhodes discussed the need for more space. It was getting close to the time to do something about it. They had some plans drawn up but no dates were set for construction.

# *Chapter Sixteen*

For the first time, Jimmy really got involved in the finances of the clinic. The property the clinic had was paid for. Dr. Rhodes had never sent out a bill. Most of the patients either paid when they came in or they had insurance. Others paid when they could. Some never paid at all. This was fine with the doctor but it wasn't all that helpful when dealing with bankers.

They needed almost one million dollars for the addition. With what funds they had they would still have to borrow almost five hundred thousand. The bank said for them to lend that amount of money the doctor would have to set up a normal billing system. He said, "Hell no."

They put together a letter and mailed it to all of his patients. It stated what they wanted to do and why they wanted to do it. They mentioned the only way they could do it was to change their billing or to come up with the money. They said they would ask just this one time for those who owed the money to pay if they could. For those who didn't owe, could they possibly make a donation? This would help the clinic give them better treatment. It would also be credited to their account and applied to future services.

The response was overwhelming. Construction would begin and there would be no need for help from the bank. People had been coming in for weeks and giving what they could. Several of the businessmen in town had donated to the clinic with no strings attached. Everyone in that town knew how important it was to keep the clinic open and up to date. Some of the mines even made a donation.

Things were a little hectic while the clinic was being enlarged. The old part of the building was being remodeled as well.

When it was all finished Jimmy decided to take a couple days off and spend it with his family. The twins were now two. The weather was great. Jimmy called Mr. Freeman to see if he could bring his family for an outing while he did a little fishing. Mr. Freeman, as usual, was agreeable.

Carol packed a picnic basket and they drove up the mountain. She had never seen a farm. She was taken back by its view and natural beauty. She spread some blankets by the stream for the twins. Jimmy headed out to fish.

Mrs. Freeman walked over where Carol was sitting with the kids and they had a chat. Later she invited them over to her house. They packed everything in the car and walked over to the house. It set on a small rise. From the front porch you could see all the way down the valley. You could see parts of Franklin. In the opposite direction there were the fields, the barns and the stream. Carol could not remember ever seeing a nicer place. Mrs. Freeman showed her the inside of the house. Carol loved it! It had four bedrooms and two baths upstairs. There was a master bedroom and a bath and a half downstairs. The rest of the rooms downstairs were large and had a view. Carol mentioned that for a house it's age she was surprised to see a master bedroom downstairs. Mrs. Freeman said that her husband added it on for her as a wedding present. She said with a smile on her face that he wanted them to be a little ways from the children at night.

The fishermen had returned. They had kept enough for dinner that night. Mr. Freeman was with them. Carol told Jimmy how much she liked the place. When they were driving home he said he loved the place himself. He said that Mr. Freeman had told him that it was getting too to be much for him and his wife. One of his sons had done very well and had been after them to sell the farm and move in with them. He said he wasn't ready just then but probably in a couple of years he would take his son up on his offer.

Carol asked Jimmy what he said to him. He said he told him he wasn't sure where he could get the money, but he would like Mr. Freeman to give him a chance to try when he decided to sell. He said he would. Carol asked how much money he thought they would need? He said he didn't know but it was a hell of alot more than they had.

That evening after the picnic they had just put the kids to bed when Dr. Rhodes arrived at their door. He was carrying a book with him like he usually did. Susan opened the door and he came right in and went straight to

Jimmy in the living room. Jimmy greeted him and asked him what brought him out so late in the evening? Smiling, the doctor said, "Will you humor an old man and take off your shoes. I want to see your feet."

Jimmy asked him why?

"Just do it, please."

Jimmy complied. He was sitting on the couch. The doctor told him to put his feet up on the coffee table. He looked at the bottom of his feet and said, "I'll be damned."

Jimmy said, "What the hell is going on?"

The doctor asked Carol for a mirror and reflected Jimmy's feet back to him. There under the smallest toes under each foot were the letters J.T. They were small but readable. He said that he had never noticed them. "Who the hell would?" said the doctor.

Jimmy asked again. "What the hell is going on?" The doctor told him to read the tenth chapter of the book he was carrying. While he was reading Hilda and Bob, whom the doctor had called, arrived.

Jimmy finished his reading. He put the book down and stared at the wall.

The doctor explained to the others.

"Over twenty years ago, Hilda had a baby that died. On her way home from the clinic she found a baby in a basket. She brought the baby back to me and she explained how she found it. Now I know she left a few items out of her story or maybe I didn't hear her right. The basket she found was attached to a small parachute. Hilda thought it might have been some sheets or maybe didn't know what a parachute looked like.

She asked me if she could keep the boy to replace the one she lost. I told her she could keep it for the time being while I tried to find out who it belonged to. If I was able to find out I would have to tell them and she would have to give up the baby. I knew that no one locally had a baby that age that was missing. Finally, I gave up looking. I filed a birth certificate for her and to this day everyone but the two of us thought he was Jimmy Willow."

Jimmy said to Hilda, "Why didn't you tell me?"

"Tell you what?" she said. "That you were left in a basket. That you were not loved. That you did not know who your mother was. What should I have told you, Jimmy? I told you the most important thing that you ever needed to know. That I loved you and I always will. To this day nothing has changed."

The doctor went on to say that he remembered the plane crash. They must have known the plane was going down and tried to save him. Then he thought he should read the entire article from the book so everyone would know what was going on. The book was about families who had left large estates to their children. Jimmy's real family had been one of those mentioned in the book. A trust fund from the family fortune had been set up for him and one other person. They were the last two surviving relatives. The fund was set up almost thirty years ago. At the time it was established it had more than three hundred million dollars in it. The book was two years old and it said the fund was now approaching four billion. It was to be paid when the youngest reached age thirty. The two of them were the same age. Just days apart. It would be paid in about six months.

Jimmy felt like his head was going to blow up. He said he liked his life just as it was. He wasn't sure he would like the change this would bring. They looked at him like he was crazy. He said as an example, "Can you imagine the people coming into the clinic. They would be coming to see that billion dollar man. I would probably have to have full time lawyers just to defend myself from charges brought against my practice. I need to think about this and I beg each of you not to say a word to anyone.

The doctor could see the stress on Jimmy's face. He mentioned one last thing as he was leaving. With that new testing it would be easy to establish who he was.

Jimmy had a hard time sleeping that night. He was not sure he wanted an instant wealth and all that he felt went along with it. He still wasn't sure what he was going to do as he walked to work the next morning. It was on his mind so much during the day that he hoped he was taking proper care of his patients. He needed to talk to Dr. Rhodes. It was his day off. Jimmy called him at home. He agreed to come over to the clinic about quitting time.

Jimmy was waiting in his office when the doctor arrived. Everyone had already gone for the day so they could talk He said, "Doc, I really don't know what I want to do. I'm leaning toward forgetting the whole thing."

The doctor said, "Jimmy, do you really know what you are doing? Do you know what the money represents?"

"What do you mean?"

He answered that the money meant freedom.

Jimmy said, "I have all the freedom I want and need." The doctor looked a little mad as he answered.

"You have some freedom now, Jimmy. How much freedom did you have when you lived in the hollow? Tell me, did you have the freedom to move from the hollow? Why not? It was because your family was poor. How many vacations did you take when you were growing up? You were not  free to take vacations, you had no money. How did you get to school? There was no way in hell you would be sitting where you are if people had not helped you with the money. They gave you the freedom to go to school, did they not?"

"Let me give you two real life examples. There was a man who came to this clinic many times. He had a family with five kids. A better man I have never known in my life. He worked hard in the mines but he couldn't make enough to give his family the basics. He went to the boss at the mine and asked if there was any additional work he could do on his hours off to make more money. There was very little his boss could help him with. In his search for additional work he came by here to see if there was anything he could do for the clinic. That summer, among other things, he painted the clinic. In the summer he cut the grass. In the winter he cut wood and shoveled snow. After the children were grown it took him two years to save the money to pay off his bill here.

I didn't want it but he wouldn't have it any other

way. This poor man gave up much of his freedom for his family. Even with all he had done and no one could have done more with what he had to work with, I've seen this man cry because he could not do more.

Money is freedom, Jimmy. Look at our politicians. They pass a tax that is only fifty dollars a month. What's the big deal? Most families could suck it up and handle it. Here's what the big deal is. Fifty dollars a month comes to six hundred dollars a year. In ten years its six thousand dollars. Then think of twenty and thirty years. At thirty years, with interest that could be more than fifty thousand dollars. Now here is where your freedom comes home. If you have it you can be free to send one of your children to college. If you don' have it maybe you can't. Another example, if your parents needed your help to get into an old folks home, it could mean the difference between a nice facility and a snake pit. If you had none of these or other needs, you could keep it for another fifteen years until you retire. At that time you would have about one hundred twenty-five thousand to add to your retirement. Do you think that would add any freedom to how you lived in retirement? You bet. That tax is only fifty bucks a month, right? No, its not. With every tax dollar that is taken, you lose a little freedom.

Now let's take the senator from Massachusetts. He has been free all of his life. He never had to worry about grocery money. He never has to work extra hours to earn money to buy milk for one of his babies. He was free to go to any school that would have him. Even then he got kicked out of one of them for cheating. Since he has never had to worry about money he cannot see how anyone else could be upset when he raises their taxes. At a party where there was alot of drinking he left with a girl in his car. He drove her into the water. He got out of the car leaving her in the car, underwater. He then swam to the mainland and went to his motel room. He didn't even report it until the following day. What do you think Joe six pack would have gotten for doing something like that? Time, lots of time. He got what amounted to a traffic ticket.

Money, Jimmy, what does it mean? To me, it's freedom. In the hands of an asshole, money can buy him anything. He can even buy freedom."

To you, Jimmy, with help you have basically freed yourself. Look around you. Can you see any use for it? Lord knows I can." With that the doctor got up and left.

Jimmy had another sleepless night. But this time he had a plan. He asked the doctor, Hilda and Bob to met him at the clinic. Again the meeting was after closing. After they all got there Jimmy said he had a plan that he needed their help with. He had decided to try and get the money. However there were a few conditions. First, he did not want want anyone to know who he was. Second, he wanted Bob to represent him. Third, he wanted the doctor, Hilda and Bob to go to Pittsburgh with him. Hilda and the doctor could tell their story about finding him. The doctor could make whatever arrangements were necessary to see that the proper testing for his identification was done. Bob would present him as John Thompson. He wouldn't give his present name. All dealings after the initial contact would be made by Bob.

If he got the money he would leave it at the bank in his own trust. They had invested it well over the past thirty years so there was no reason to change it now. Bob would be in charge of the trust. He didn't know for sure but he thought the trust could earn more than one hundred million dollars a year.

Jimmy said, "Doctor, that could be a hell of alot of freedom."

He said, "Don't you know it?"

After things settled down he wanted Bob and the doctor to work for the trust full time. Everyone agreed. They started to plan their trip to Pittsburgh. Bob had called the trust. As he expected they were not receptive. After several phone calls they agreed to see them.

When they arrived in Pittsburgh they went straight to the bank where they were greeted and taken to a large reception room. They had a total of six men there. They started to ask some questions. Then Bob said, "Why don't I let Dr. Rhodes tell you the story?"

They listened but they didn't seem to care much for what he said. They said they had expected that some people would be coming forward. Since that book had come out there had been two others. Jimmy took off his shoes and showed his feet. They said that others had done that also. Two of the men in the room were doctors. They said they would need a sample of Jimmy's blood. They had already prepared the samples to match it because of the other cases.

Dr. Rhodes said that would be fine but he also would like to have certification they were comparing it to was the real article. Then he said that if the samples didn't match he wanted an independent comparison made. They agreed.

They were only in Pittsburgh two hours when they were heading home. They had been told it would take a few weeks for the testing to be completed.

The time dragged on three weeks, then four. Bob went to Pittsburgh to see what the story was. They didn't answer but from the looks on their faces he knew he was right. They said it would be just a few more days.

Back at home, Bob thought he should not get everyone's hopes up so he said it would be just a couple more days. While he was in Pittsburgh he spent time with the bankers playing what if. They were in agreement that they would keep the trust and manage it. Everyone was aware that it would require a mountain of paperwork but that it could be done. They said off the record that the fund was at four billion four hundred million. Bob thought it a little strange that the other relative didn't show up or protest the findings.

A few days later Bob was notified that the tests were back. They confirmed that he was in fact John Thompson. The funds would be turned over in three months.

During that three months, Jimmy, Bob and Dr. Rhodes spent days planning. They decided that Bob and the doctor would work for the trust full time. The trust in turn would pay each of them one hundred thousand dollars per year to help and keep some order in their office in the garage. Hilda decided to work for the trust as well.

They had to set up some rules. They didn't intend to help anyone who did not want to help themselves. Because of the clinic they knew everyone in town. They surely knew the ones who were having a rough time.

To get additional information Hilda came up with a new form that all people who came into the clinic had to fill out. There were a few complaints but they said the information was for a study that they were conducting and it could help some people at a later date. With this form in a period of two months they knew more about people than they really wanted to. They knew who owed money on their homes, cars and who had large credit card balances or other debts. Of course they knew who owed the clinic money.

After all this was added up the amount it came to would put just a little dent into the trust.

The doctor told Jimmy he didn't know what they could do with all that money. Jimmy said, "Doctor, you told me you wanted freedom. Is too much of anything a good thing?"

That night they let their minds expand. They could give money to the school. They could help the with the sports program, the band and they send the good students to college. They thought teacher incentive pay might be good or just giving more pay to the teachers overall.

They tried to think of ways of giving the people help that they couldn't screw up. As an example, if they gave money for teachers pay overall then the county might feel that they could lower the amount they were paying. They did not want to pay someone's loan off if he had a drinking problem. That would just enable them to drink more. They would need to get him dried out first. It appeared there was more to this money giving than they had thought.

Soon after, the trust transfer was a done deal. Jimmy said he would prefer not to spend much time with it. Because the doctor was working with Bob now, he was taking on the full load at the clinic.

Bob and the doctor put the word out that they were looking for another doctor for the clinic. Jimmy didn't know what they were doing until he saw the salary they were willing to pay. If they found a new doctor he would be well paid. About half of his pay would come from the trust. Jimmy said, "Why the hell not, it's freedom, right doctor?"

The next thing Bob and the doctor did was hire a real estate agent and an engineer. They didn't tell Jimmy what it was all about.

The young girl who had given her twins away came into the clinic one day. She wanted to speak to Jimmy. As fate would have it Carol came to the clinic at the same time with the twins. They had met and talked in the reception area.

The young girl spoke to Jimmy. She said that she

wanted to see him before leaving town. The kids in town and at school had found out about her having the babies and they would just not let it rest. She said she wanted to stop by and tell him that she felt she had made the right decision about the babies. She also wanted to thank him for his help. As she was leaving she said she hoped her babies were with a family as nice as his. The way she looked at him he got the feeling she knew. She knew and approved.

# *Chapter Seventeen*

There had been a rumor that some one was buying up land in the hollow and other places. No one paid much attention to this as the mine companies had been doing this for years. They would buy up a large parcel of land and put a mine under it.

Two more years had passed. The twins were four years old and doing well. Little Jimmy was fourteen and finishing his first year in high school. He wasn't setting the world on fire but he was a good student.

Kathy would be finishing her training in one year. She and Jimmy talked and she wanted to work in the clinic when she finished with her internship. She had turned out to be a G.P. as well.

Kathy had found a guy she was serious about. They were planning to get married when she was finished with her studies. Jimmy had met him once. His name was Harry. Kathy met him while she was in medical school. Jimmy thought he was a nice man.

Bob had been able to convince Mike to complete college. It was tough at times. His heart wasn't in it but he hung in there and made it. He was now going to do what he wanted. That was go to art school. Big Zero had paid for much of his college and now it was doing well enough to pay for his art classes.

Jimmy and Bob had talked about the trust helping out Kathy and Mike. He said he preferred it the way it was. He said they were doing alot of growing up and he liked it that way.

Bobby had been home a few months ago. He was doing great. He had received his first star. He was now a Rear Admiral. He said he felt he was being lined up to take over the submarine development program in a few years.

Susan and the children looked like they should have their picture in some magazine. They were a good looking family. Susan was doing a super job of raising them.

Dr. Rhodes had not worked in the clinic now for two years. He was almost seventy-five years old. It was starting to show. Jimmy had asked him to come by the clinic on more than one occasion. He said that it wasn't necessary. He had told Jimmy when you get to his age the only big question left in life was what you were going to die from. Each time the he made that statement, Jimmy realized just how much this man meant to his life and so many others.

The doctor who was hired for the clinic was doing a good job. He mentioned to Jimmy that he didn't know how a small clinic could pay him the amount of salary he was getting.. He had informed Jimmy from the beginning that it was his intention to work there for a few years and then to start a practice of his own. He needed to pay off loans he had from going to school and he wanted to save some money to set up his own place. Jimmy talked him into staying one more year until Kathy could be there. He offered him a little something extra, with the help of Bob, so he would have a little additional set up money

Several things were starting to happen. There had been a new section of government highway planned for some time. It was to come through area about twenty miles from Franklin. Now it was under construction and it was about one mile from Franklin. Jimmy asked Bob how this could happen? He said, "You don't want to know."

Jimmy wondered what impact the new highway would have on the clinic. It was completed about the time Kathy returned to work there. What had been a little too much for one doctor was getting to be too much for two.

It was announced that the state had decided to build a new junior college in Franklin. Some local person who wanted to remain anonymous had donated the land. It was this donation that made up their minds. Franklin was selected since such a high percentage of students from the two local high school were going on to college. Also it was chosen because the new highway made the area more accessible. Further, when the first class reached their third year, the school would be expanded to a four year school.

Jimmy talked to Bobby about the school. As he suspected the trust had donated the land. The very last bit of doubt that he had about the use of the money was gone. He saw what they were doing and he was pleased.

Now with the highway and the school, two small electronic companies were in the process of locating there. They would each have about one hundred fifty workers. There was also a good source of labor in the area for them.

When the new school was built part of their responsibilities would be to retrain the miners as the mines continued to be worked out or closed.

The area was taking on a new life. People seemed happy. For the first time in years new homes were being built. Building in the area had become almost a lost art. People were also starting to remodel and fix up their homes.

The bank that had complained because so many of its loans were paid off was doing plenty of new business. They were also financing business loans. This was something they had not done in years.

Bob was also on the board of the bank. The trust had paid off so many loans that he thought for awhile that the bank might have a problem. Now the people exercised their new freedom and they were doing better than ever.

Pressure was on at the clinic. With the load they had now Jimmy couldn't see them being able to handle the traffic when the new school was up and running. Also, with the new business that would be there shortly, something had to be done now.

They had the plans prepared. The new addition would enable them to more than double their capacity. They figured that they would need three more doctors. Not all at once but over the next few years. They decided to branch out. Jimmy and Kathy would be the only G.P.'s. The others would specialize. The new facility would also have a dental wing and an eye clinic. It was nice to know where the money would go. It would be built in stages with total completion in approximately three years.

Jimmy, as he loved to do, was spending the afternoon at Mr. Freeman's farm. The fishing was as good as ever. He took a break from fishing and sat on the creek bank. He opened his thermos and was drinking a a cup of coffee when Mr. Freeman came by. Jimmy invited him to sit and join him.

The two friends sat there and talked. Jimmy asked Mr. Freeman how much longer he thought he would be staying on the farm. He said it would not be much longer now. Jimmy asked him how much he wanted for the farm. He said he didn't feel that he could discuss it at that time.

Jimmy got the feeling he was trying to avoid the answer. Coming in, Jimmy noticed what looked like a new house being built. He asked Mr. Freeman about it. He said that a real estate agent said it might be better if the farm had a place where employees and their families could live.

On the way home Jimmy thought what was going on there didn't make sense. On second thought, maybe it would be better to have the extra house for the hands.

When Jimmy got home he talked to Carol about what happened at the Freeman farm. By the way she acted, she appeared to have changed her mind about the place. They had looked forward to buying it since they had originally seen it. He thought all they were doing was waiting for Mr. Freeman to say when. They were still living in the small house he had bought shortly after finishing school. He thought she would be in a hurry to get out of it by now. He was puzzled by her change of heart.

There was alot of blasting going on in the hollow. Someone had bought up the land and it looked like they were clearing much of it. He asked Bob about it, then he said it must be a mining outfit. Bob said, "You could be right."

The work had been going on for a couple of months. They had contoured the entire hollow and even built a dam on the creek. The blasting they had heard at first was the old mine entrances being blasted shut.

It seems that when oxygen is removed from being exposed to the minerals, the water that filters out of the mines is all right. It is the oxygen working with minerals that causes the acid to form.

With heavy equipment they had cleaned out the creek beds as well. The water now would be clean enough for things to live and for the animals to drink.

When they cleaned out the hollow most of the trees were saved. Now they went back in and planted additional trees. Many of the new trees were fruit and nut trees. They would be beautiful when they were in blossom. The creek had been channeled so the water would run slower but deeper. Several one or two acre parks had been built with benches and picnic areas around them.

Jimmy had been watching this for months. After work one day he stopped to see Bob and as expected he had his hand in it. Jimmy had figured as much. So far Jimmy had liked what he had seen. He asked Bob to fill him in on what the project was going to look like when it was finished?

Bob said, "You told me you didn't want to be involved in this thing on a day to day basis. Well, just let me tell you that you will like the finished product. Now why don't you just wait and see it?"

"Well, at least tell me how much longer it will take?"

"Haste makes waste, my boy," he said.

Jimmy knew he wasn't going to get an answer. He also knew he trusted Bob without question. It looked like he as well as many others would just have to wait and see.

Occasionally, Jimmy would go out to the hollow and see what was happening. Every time he figured what they had in mind, they would take another left turn. The last time he was out there they had even paved the old dirt road. Now it was a nice two lane street. There were also paved parking areas along the street. He could drive almost to the end of the hollow. He parked his car at the last paved parking area. He walked up stream a little way to where he heard some equipment working. They were almost finished building a dam across the creek. He went up on the side of the hill and watched them for about twenty minutes.

The way they had cleared the land behind the dam, it looked like it would be twenty-five feet deep and cover the entire hollow. The dam would be about one hundred acres. It would be great for the people of the town to go fishing and boating. Another road came down from the top of the dam where you could put a boat in. As he was about to leave he remembered the tunnel. He thought he should mention that to them. He was afraid some children might get hurt playing in it. As he walked to his car he looked over to where the opening for the tunnel had been. There was a large pipe running into the hill. The tunnel was closed.

He remembered why the tunnel was originally was built. The next valley over was going to be getting the water they had been waiting on for so many years. That would make the land much more valuable. He was glad for Carol's father. His farm was one of the biggest in the valley.

Back at the clinic, things were a disorganized mess with the addition being built. One of the things Jimmy enjoyed doing was looking at the hollow once a month or so just to observe the development progress.

Jimmy and Carol lived in a small five room house. He thought about putting on an addition. Carol had been against that because she didn't like the location that well. He decided he would look for a place on his own and maybe surprise her. He had looked a couple times but nothing turned him on. He was about to give up. Then he mentioned it to Carol. She had been after him about the house for several years. Now, for some reason, she didn't seem to be in a hurry.

It had been several weeks since his last trip to the

hollow. He and Carol had talked about the project several times. He had told her about the water going through the tunnel. She said with more than a little pride that it was her idea. Since they were already committed to the dam she thought it only made sense to put it in the plumbing. She had told her father. He was excited about it coming. He said the water would make the farms more productive. It was a shame that so many farmers had left their farms over the years. Now they would have been able to make a go of it.

Carol said her father told her that someone had bought up most of the old farms. That bothered Jimmy. He thought that maybe someone knew what they were going to do and was taking advantage of things. He stopped by to see Bob. Bob said that he knew that someone was buying up the farms. Further he said he knew who it was. It was the trust. He said since they were responsible for the increase in value they should share in it. Also, since they were buying the land at such a low price they could sell it to the right families at a very good value.

Once again Jimmy was impressed with Bob. He knew that he had been one step above most people since he had met him.

Jimmy decided to stop by the hollow on his way back to the clinic. He was astonished. Since he was there last the whole place had come alive. The trees had turned green. Grass covered the ground. There was clean water in the creek. He thought the dam must be full. He didn't have time then to run up to the hollow and see it. However, at the beginning of where the old dirt road used to start, they had carved the area up into a park. There were three baseball fields. They were different sizes for different age groups. There was a soccer field as well. Each of the fields had covered stands for people to sit in. There was plenty of parking space and even a concession building. Every-was fenced in. The grass was just taking hold but the rest was complete.

When Jimmy got to the clinic he called Bob at his office. The doctor was there as well. He told them that what they had done to that piece of crap was nothing short of a miracle. He said it was a shame that no one would ever know it was them. The doctor got on the phone. You could hear his age in his voice on the phone. He said, "Jimmy, it is not a miracle, it is the freedom you have given this town. Now the kids will have the freedom to play ball. Maybe someday, someone who got his start on that field will make it to the big leagues. Won't that be fantastic?"

Bob got back on the phone and told Jimmy that he had to go to Pittsburgh with him. Part of the trust agreement required that they visit with bankers at least once every five years. The time had come. He had been assured by the bank that their coming and going would be kept under wraps so as not to cause Jimmy any publicity. They agreed to go the following Friday.

The last of the work for enlarging the clinic was finalized. Kathy had taken on the job of screening the new doctors. They were up to staff. Both the dentist office and the eye clinic were up and running. All the clinic did for them was rent them space. It was nice to have the clinic up to speed again. The individual work load would now be at an acceptable level.

Jimmy was looking forward to getting away for a day or so even if it was a business trip. They had planned on staying one night in Pittsburgh and being on the road back by noon.

_____

# *Chapter Eighteen*

Kathy and Harry Reid who she met in medical school announced they were going to get married. Harry, was a lawyer and he had been in town for several months setting up an office. Other than Bob he was the only lawyer in town. During this time he had gotten to know the family.

It was good to see Kathy and Bob get together. They seemed to make a nice couple. They were planning their wedding in two months.

On the drive to Pittsburgh, Jimmy and Bob planned to go over what they had done with the trust over the past five years. This would make good use of the time and keep them busy going. On their way back they were going to try to give some direction to what they wanted to do in the future.

Bob had brought a pile of files that he was going to review with Jimmy. Jimmy was driving. Jimmy asked Bob the question, "Do you think anyone in Franklin has figured out what is going on yet?"

He said to the best of his knowledge they had not. A few people knew he was involved in it in some way but they thought he was just acting as a lawyer in the matter. He said if it had gotten out they would have heard about it.

People would be coming in and asking for money.

They started on the list. First, they went over all the loans and credit cards they had paid off. When this was done the people who were helped were told that this was a one time deal. By accepting the money, they agreed in the future to pay their credit cards within thirty days and not to borrow on their homes again. This had amounted to quite a sum of of money. However, the pot they were dealing with was quite large,

There were at least one thousand people who had been helped by having their credit paid off. Rather than go over each one Bob just covered those who didn't live up to their side of the deal or where something had gone wrong. As an example, some of the people changed their lifestyle quite a bit. This was the freedom that they had hoped to give them. However they also had given them the ability to do some stupid things. One couple who had two children who were about to go to college did this. They lived in a house that they had borrowed the maximum on. They had an old pick-up truck that was on its last legs. With their new freedom they bought two new expensive cars. The payments on the two new cars were higher than the one on the house had been.

Another couple sold their house to their son. He had never left home. They got another large loan on the house. This time the loan was in the son's name. They felt that way they did not break the agreement they had made to get their house loan paid off. There were a couple of dozen cases like this. Another couple who had credit cards only in the husband's name had them paid off. Then they went out and got cards in the wife's name. These cards were now charged to the maximum. The two claimed they had lived up to the agreement. Jimmy told Bob that some of these people would make good lawyers.

For the most part those who had been helped had lived up to the agreement. You could see the difference in them as they started to exercise good judgment with the new freedom this gave them.

Jimmy asked about the highway location. Bob gave him the same answer. "You really don't want to know."

The teacher program had been a big success. On average the top one-half of the teachers in the nine schools of the district were receiving from three to ten thousand dollars a year. Bob had worked out a deal with the head of the district school system. They set up goals for the teachers based on classroom and overall performance. The trust paid for one full time person who reported to the head man and the trust. It was that persons job to review teacher performance and rate them among their peers.

The long term effect of this program had really taken hold. The poorer teachers were identified as well as the good. The school system was better able to work on the low end of the group now that they were identified. The new teacher selection was great. The incentive plan had gotten out. The district was first choice for better teachers who were coming into the system. Those teachers worked harder for the money and recognition. The district had gone from the middle of the pack to the top in the state.

The next topic was some of the new business that had come to town. It seems the trust, in some cases, had given long term ground leases at very good rates. In others the land was given free. The net effect of this rather small investment was the virtual elimination of unemployment. It had also enabled the town to grow more than twice its size. People were moving in at a steady rate of four or five families in a month. That had enabled the people of Franklin to really improve their quality of life.

Next, they talked about the college program they had set up for the kids. Bob hired a full time person who worked for the district head. She administers the program Before coming to work for the trust, she was a principal at one of the district schools. She loved her job and she was good at it. If a kid was qualified and accepted in college, she saw that the bills got paid.

The program was simple. If you maintained a B average or better you could go to a state school. If you were in the top five percent of the class you could go to any school that would accept you.

Last year over ninety percent of the children went to college. Some schools knowing that these kids were good payers (the trust) sent recruiters to the two high schools. This program was doing great.

Along with the teachers program, it would be exciting to watch the on going improvement. When the kids had more years with better teachers and the hope of going to college based on their grades, it was going to be something to view with pride.

Next, Jimmy wanted to know how the college got there.

"Well," Bob said, "once we finished the highway deal, we started to talk about college for as many kids as possible. We figured if we couldn't send them all to school, why not bring the school here? We talked to the state authorities. At first, they didn't approve the idea. We told them that we would donate five hundred acres at the interchange on the new highway. That made them listen. Further, we offered to fund two positions on the college staff. Still they could not make up their minds. Finally, we agreed to upgrading the local schools to ensure that at least one-half of the students would go to college. At the time only twenty percent were going. If we didn't reach that level we agreed to fund that many students from other areas of the state to bring the combined number up to fifty percent. We had five years to reach that goal and we exceeded it.

The state people agreed to the school and we gave them the land. There was one more condition. If in the future the local area needed some land for a school at that location, they would let them have it.

If you remember we hired two people full time when we started. One was an engineer and the other was a real estate man. This was one of the real estate man's first projects. We knew the highway was coming and where the exchange would be. He bought up all four corners. At the time most of the land was just waste land. After the highway came in we gave the state land for the school. Then he sold one of the other corners for a restaurant, a hamburger place, a gas station, a hardware store and a strip center with a supermarket. He made enough profit to pay back the trust for all four corners. We are holding the remaining corners out for possible industrial use."

The last item to discuss was the hollow. Bob said that was where the engineer came in. They had been doing things for individual people. It was having a good effect. Now they wanted to do something that would benefit the entire town.

The hollow had always been rather open. No one lived there for a number of years. There were just falling down shacks and that acid creek. At one time years ago the place had even been used as a dump. No one ever went there.

They thought if they could take that area and make it into something the whole town would be proud of they would have accomplished something.

The engineer worked for two months checking on elevations, closed mine entrances and on the tunnel. Carol thought of the tunnel. While he was doing that, Mister Real Estate was putting the land package together. There were several owners. Many had moved out of state and were one or more generations removed from the original owner. A number of properties had been claimed by the county for back taxes.

Finally it was all put together. The trust owned all

the land from where the dirt road started all the way up the hollow and then to the property line with Mr. Freeman. In addition they had bought the hill that the tunnel went through. They also now owned most of the old farms in the valley where Carol was from.

The work started from the top down. They blasted the mines shut first. That put a stop to the acid water. Bob said, "You know, all that blasting only cost about two thousand dollars. It could have been done years ago. What a waste!. There hadn't been an operating mine in that hollow for at least thirty years. All that time that water could have been cleaned up.

Then they cleared the area of most of the junk. They cleaned out the old creek bed and buried it on the side of the hill. The type of trees they planted would, in the years to come, supply food for the wild animals. Once that lower area was cleared and planted, they went back up the hollow and started the dam. The engineer had planned the dam as a park like setting for the people from Franklin to use. He thought it would be good for picnicking as well as fishing and boating. Taking the water through the tunnel was Carol's idea and that made sense.

With the hollow project done they started on the sports complex. Here they would have liked to do a few more things but they ran out of space.

The dam and the sports complex were intended to be self-supporting. At the dam there would be a one dollar admittance fee. There would also be a boat rental fee. All of this was on the honor system. One could just drive to the dam. At the dam there was a piece of paper to fill out and a container to put the money in. The same with the boats. No private boats were allowed. Only paddle boats were permitted. When you took a boat you left a dollar.

The farmers over in the valley would be charged a small fee for the water. It would be just enough to keep the plumbing working. None of the original cost was factored into the bill. The system was run by valves. There were no pumps, therefore the cost was very low.

There was a small charge suggested for all adults who attended the games at the sports complex. It was twenty-five cents or a donation for up keep. All paying was on the honor system."

As they were approaching Pittsburgh, Jimmy asked how much all of this had cost? He knew that the clinic had used over fifteen million for its enlargement. Bob said he wasn't sure he knew right to the penny. He suggested that they wait to see the bankers. They would have all that information.

They stopped for lunch before they headed over to the bank. Over lunch, they talked about the doctor. He was to the point he was not really doing much. That didn't bother either of them. What bothered Bob was that he was having trouble keeping up with it himself. Not that he minded the work. He just couldn't keep up the pace. They talked about adding another person. Possibly the bank could recommend someone to them. They discussed Harry, Kathy's husband to be. That had two possible draw-backs. First, if they chose Harry and he wanted the job, they would also have to tell Kathy. Then six people would know. They left the question open for more discussion.

They got to the bank at one-thirty. They were taken into a large conference room. There were three bank employees in the room with them. They had all kinds of computer runs which they discussed mostly with Bob.

One of the charts they showed listed all the things that the fund's money was invested in. They said they thought the fund had done well during the past five years. The fund had spent almost two hundred million dollars. In that same period the fund had earned over eight million. It was now worth six hundred million more than it was in the beginning. Frankly, they weren't surprised. However, just seeing what all the money was doing back in Franklin made you think the pile was going down.

They were asked to give a rough projection on how much they would be spending in the up coming year. They said if they had a better idea of what they were up against as far as spending was concerned, they might be able to invest it a little better. Bob said he would be back in touch with them.

Jimmy thought it didn't seem worthwhile to make a trip for such a short meeting. He thought it could have been handled over the phone.

When they were leaving as they were waiting for the elevator to close Bob said, "We spend two hundred million and that's not enough. How about that!"

Just before the elevator door closed, one of the men from the bank asked them to wait. He handed Jimmy a bag. He said that the other relative who got the other half of the trust had left it for him. He said his cousin knew that he wanted to maintain his privacy but thought he might like to have the contents of the bag. He said further that if he had any questions he could give him a call. His telephone number was in the bag. The bank employee saw the look on Jimmy's face and told him if he wanted to return something to him and not meet him, he would be glad to be the go between." Jimmy thanked him and they left.

That evening back at the hotel they talked about the trust for a short time. One thing for sure, they were not spending it fast enough. They agreed to wait until the next day on the ride home to talk about any changes they might want to make.

The bag that Jimmy had been given was burning him alive with curiosity. He managed to put off opening it until after dinner. Back in the room he could wait no longer. He opened the bag. Inside was a collection of things that belonged to his real mother and father. Bob, seeing how this was affecting him decided to give him some time alone. He left the room and went to the lobby bar for a drink.

Jimmy looked over what he had been given. It did not seem like much but it was alot. He had never seen a picture of his real mother and father before. There were other news articles about the family and the plane crash. His father's doctorate degree was there. A picture of the house where they lived. A picture of his grandparents.

There was his mother's wedding ring that was found at the crash site. The last thing he looked at was a note and a picture from the sender. The picture seemed to be a few years old considering they were the same age. Whatever, he looked like a nice man. He went on to say that both of his parents were gone now as well. They had kept those articles at their home for many years. He said he never thought that he would get them someday. He said further that he hoped he was well and that his sending him these articles didn't offend him.

Jimmy put everything away and laid back on the bed. He thought about the man who sent him these things. He was his only living relative if he had no children. He seemed like a nice man. He wondered if he should contact him.

Bob found Jimmy asleep on the bed with his clothes on when he got back to the room. He took his shoes off, pulled the covers over him and left him that way.

Jimmy got up during the night and took his clothes off. They both got a good night's sleep. After a light early breakfast, they were on the road by eight in the morning.

As planned, the subject of the trust was the main topic of discussion. It was evident that they would have to expand the area of and the size of the operation. The man at the bank said they would be making over two hundred fifty million a year. That was more than they had spent in the last five years. What the hell else could they do and how could they do it?

Bob said that he had been thinking about this last night. They needed to build a fire wall between them and the money. Jimmy asked what he meant? He suggested that they create a corporation that might even be out of the country. Everything would pass through it and no one would be able to find out who was behind it.

Jimmy said, "I don't know. This whole thing sounds like it is getting out of hand."

"Don't give up that easy, Jimmy. If we go ahead and add one more person, let's say Harry, to the group we could with just a couple more people in the school system expand the teacher and scholarship program to the entire county. This could eat up millions as you know. I think it is the most successful thing that we have done."

Bob went over some other things he had been thinking of working on. As an example, he thought they could improve the high school sports program. They could build each high school a new gym and sports complex. The local college needed more dorms. They also needed a sports facility. The city hall in Franklin was on its last legs, etc. By the time they got back to town, Bob had convinced Jimmy to hang in there.

As they drove into Franklin Bob told Jimmy that they were to meet Carol and the kids at their house for lunch. He had forgotten to tell him sooner.

In the years since he and Carol had been married, this was the first night they had been apart. When they drove up to Hilda's house Carol must have felt like he did. She came running outside to the car and gave him a big hug. The kids were right behind her. He knew and felt how lucky he was. It was good to see them.

They had such a nice lunch at Hilda's. At lunch Carol told Jimmy she would like to talk to him. It was a Saturday. She asked him if they could drive over to the office and chat there. Hilda agreed to watch the children. On the way to the office Carol started talking about this and that. Finally, she got around to what Jimmy thought was the main topic. She said that she wanted a new house. After thinking it over she thought they should buy the Freeman farm. Jimmy said, "Well, that's just fine. What do you think Mr. Freeman will think about this?"

Carol said, Why don't we drive up there and find out?"

"That's fine but let's stop by the house so I can leave off my bags from the trip." She was way ahead of him on this one. She said they had left them at Hilda's and they would pick them up on the way back.

They talked about Mr. Freeman on the drive up to his farm. Jimmy said he hoped he was ready to sell but what did she want to do if he did not?

As they drove up to the house no one came out to greet them. They walked up to the door and rang the bell. Mrs. Freeman came to the door, greeted them and let them in. As she led them into the living room a big cheer went up. It was a surprise birthday party for Jimmy. He had almost forgotten that this was his birthday. Everybody in his family was there.

After everyone had a drink and a piece of cake

Bob got their attention. He said he had some announcements to make. First, that Mr. and Mrs. Freeman were leaving, but before they left, they had some unfinished business to take care of with Jimmy.

Mr. Freeman came over to Jimmy and handed him the keys to the farm. He said he knew how much he and Carol loved the place. He was happy that he was leaving it with them. He said that he had been sorry he was unable to leave it to one of his children. Now, however, he knew it would be in loving hands and that all he had done over his entire life would not have been wasted. Bob thanked him and he and his wife drove off to spend their remaining years with their son.

Everyone came over to Jimmy and started singing Happy Birthday again. It was sinking in to his thick head that they had bought the place.

The trip to Pittsburgh, in part, had been a diversion to get him out of town so they could move their belongings to the farm house without him knowing. She couldn't let him go to the old house and see it empty. He had been had and he loved it! He hugged Carol and said, "If a man is going to be lied to this is the way to go."

Bobby and Susan were there with their children. It was so good to see them. They were going to stay at the farm until Monday. That would give them the chance to get caught up on each other's life.

Mike had brought a girlfriend with him. They would be staying with Hilda. It was good to see Mike. He looked like he had matured quite a bit in the last few years. Jimmy had a chance to talk to him that evening. He invited him to come back to fish and a fish fry.

That evening Mike told Jimmy that he wasn't sure but he thought he was going to ask the girl he was with to marry him. He had met her back east. She was from big money. He said that was the only thing that bothered him. His life was simple. Tee shirts and a beer. She was neck ties and champagne.

Mike mentioned that he had sold off Big Zero. He was surprised that he was paid several thousand dollars for it. He said he thought he had run out of ideas for it so he might as well sell it.

Mike was now working for a large publishing house as their lead illustrator. He seemed to like what he was doing. He had arrived there a few days early and had painted them a large wall picture as a house warming gift. He had gone up on the hill where the tunnel used to come out. He had painted a view of the valley and Carol's father's farm.

That night when everyone had left or gone to bed, Jimmy and Carol got that picture and hung it on the wall across from the foot of their bed. They got in bed and looked at the picture. It was if they were back in high school. It was like they were sitting at the end of the tunnel kissing. This time there were no restrictions in love making.

The next morning Jimmy was up early but Bobby had already beat him to the punch. He was up and already had made coffee. They sat at the kitchen table and talked.

Bobby had been in the Navy for twenty years. He had received his second star. He said he would be getting his third star in a couple years. He was almost thirty-eight years old. He said he planned to retire at age fifty. He planned to have all four stars by that time.

Jimmy thought about telling Bobby about the trust. He thought if he could help them he would.

It was getting light outside. Jimmy asked Bobby if he would like to take a short drive with him. They got in Jimmy's car and drove to Franklin to where the old dirt road used to start. That was where the new sports complex started now. They drove past that and down the old hollow road. Bobby was amazed. He said, "Who in the hell did all this? It sure would have been better growing up here if this place had been like this."

They drove to the end of the road and walked up to the dam. Bobby said he had to bring his kids back there . He thought they would love it.

As they were leaving Bobby said, "You know, Jimmy, I have never brought my wife or children back to the hollow. I don't know if it was because of the way it looked or because of all the pain we experienced here."

It was still only seven when they got back to the farm. The girls had gotten up and made breakfast. There were two four wheel all terrain bikes in the barn. Jimmy and Bobby decided to use them. Jimmy said he wanted to see as much of the farm as he could. There was a perime-ter dirt road that also served as a fire break that went around most of the farm, Jimmy had no idea how big two thousand acres was. It seemed to go on forever. Someone in the recent past had put up a new perimeter fence. That made it hard for them to get lost. As they were riding they came across a couple of men working. That was the first time Jimmy had thought about how he was going to run the farm. That thought started to bother him as they rode on. The ride itself was fun.

They got back to the farm house about nine. Carol came out and Jimmy's first words to her were, "Who in the hell is going to run this farm? I don't know a dam thing about it."

Carol simply said, "I don't know."

He said, "So!"

She said, "I'm going to run the farm. Did you see the duplex that has been built? Well, that was built to be a home for the farm foreman and his helper. We had Mr. Freeman build that house as part of the purchase agreement. He also felt we needed help." The foreman had worked for Mr. Freeman for several years. Carol smiled and said that with the foreman and her supervision they would do just fine.

Jimmy and Bobby gathered up their fishing gear and headed to the ponds. They were soon joined by Mike and Dr. Rhodes.

When Jimmy and Bobby were off by themselves Bobby asked, "Where in the hell did you get the money to buy this place?"

Jimmy said, "Well, that could be a long story."

"I'll bet," Bobby replied. That bigger clinic you are

running must really be bringing in the bucks."

After all the plans were made for Kathy's wedding, she and Harry decided to run off and get married. They said they'd known each other for three years and didn't want to wait six more weeks nor did they want to go to all that expense.

Although everyone was disappointed at not sharing their big day with them, they understood their reasoning. Harry was welcomed into the family.

Jimmy and Carol settled in to their new life on the farm. They became acquainted with and liked the two men who worked there. Jimmy had a long talk with the foreman. He said they may have to hire additional help a few times a year when they were in one of their peek seasons. Jimmy knew that Mr. Freeman was right to recommend hiring these two men. He also knew that he didn't have the time it would take to properly run the farm.

Living on the farm, however, was another matter. The kids loved it. The twins each had their own pet. Jimmy Jr., as he had started being called, had a friend or two over almost every day.

The work at the clinic had settled into a routine. Kathy was spending alot more time running the clinic. This was fine with Jimmy as he preferred to spend more time with his patients. He hoped that she would officially take over management of the place.

Kathy found out she was expecting. Jimmy thought they should talk about her taking over management of the clinic, anyway. She agreed and said that she would assume the management after the baby was born.

Jimmy had a patient who was a little off the wall. Unfortunately, he was also the mayor of Franklin. Now he was running for re-election. After he had run the last time and won the people found out what a nut he was. He knew he had little chance of winning again. He was telling everybody that he knew where all the money was coming from for all the things that had been done for them. If he was re-elected he would make sure it didn't stop. When he was asked who it was he said it was a sworn secret, how could he tell?

The good mayor came to see Jimmy. He had a minor problem that was taken care of. Jimmy felt it was not in the best interests of the town that he be re-elected. While he was there Jimmy took the opportunity to talk with him. Jimmy knew that he wouldn't tell him if he asked so he said that he had heard that he really didn't know who was behind the money. The mayor said that the voters would just have to make up their minds on election day.

Jimmy was getting concerned again about the trust. If having an asshole for mayor was going to be one of the prices that had to be paid, he had his doubts.

---

# *Chapter Nineteen*

Jimmy and Bob got together to discuss the trust. Without a doubt Bob needed more than just a little help. They went over the list of projects again. A few new ones were added. One project, if they decided to do it, would be Jimmy's to handle. With what they had before them it was time to add help.

Harry and Kathy were invited to dinner. Bobby and Susan would be there as well. When dinner was over they went to the living room for what turned out to be a long evening. They went over the whole story with Harry and Kathy. For the longest time they just sat there as if they were in a trance. Finally they started asking questions. It was alot to take in at one sitting. Kathy said that she was hurt that she was just finding out. Jimmy said, "I'm not sure that you have missed much. Most of this has just been a pain in the ass if you ask me."

"As an example, the stupid mayor is running around town telling everyone that he knows who is doing all of these good deeds. If he doesn't get re-elected it all just might stop." Jimmy said he sounded like a democrat telling someone on social security that if they did not vote for them that the republicans would cut them off, or the children would have to go to school without lunch.

Kathy said, "That's no problem. I can take care of the good mayor. Just leave it to me."

Jimmy said, "What do you have in mind, sister? Remember, it can not come back to us by someone finding out what we are doing."

"Well, you will just have to wait and see. I don't think you would enjoy it half as much if you knew how it was going to happen."

They talked to Harry and he agreed to come on board. Over the next couple of months he would shut down his business and move in with them. It would not take long to complete his commitments to his clients.

They thought of renting space for an office. That might shed some light on them. While Harry was closing down the office they would add another addition on to the old garage that had been a part of the house. The garage was getting to be about the size of the house.

The project that was on the front burner at that time was expanding the teacher incentive program and the college scholarship program to the entire county.

As they were leaving Jimmy and Carol gave the keys to their old house to Kathy and Harry as a wedding present. Kathy thanked them and hugged Jimmy so hard that Carol would have been concerned if she had not been his sister. As they were getting into their car Carol remarked to Jimmy, "Isn't it nice to see someone that happy?" Jimmy said that it must be nice for her because every time he saw her she was that happy.

Bob and Jimmy stayed after the others had left.

Bob wanted him to look over the fire walls he had put in place and see what he thought.

Carol and the children went to early mass on Sunday like they usually did. Jimmy didn't go with them. He wanted some quiet time at home to work on the trust items. The pastor came to the church about two years after he and Carol were married. He and Jimmy never hit it off. Jimmy had made it a point to keep his distance from him so as to keep the peace. The mass was almost over when a young boy brought Jimmy a note. It was a request from the pastor to stay and see him after mass.

Jimmy waited out in front of the church for the pastor to come out. The alter boys and the last of the church goers had left when the pastor came out. Jimmy asked what he wanted. He said it was about time they had a talk. Jimmy asked what about? He had no idea what to expect.

Father Lima said for openers he didn't feel he was giving enough to the church. He said that with what he made he felt that his contributions left a little to be desired. Jimmy was starting to get hot. He asked how much the pastor thought he should give?

He answered, "Just like it says in the Bible, ten percent. What are you supposed to give ten percent for? For all the good works that the church does."

Jimmy said, "Like run an orphanage or a school for the kids? You closed the orphanage several years ago and the school ten years ago. But that's alright. Ten percent for good deeds seems fair to me. Let's see what I do with my money. First, I pay both ends of social security which is about twelve percent of what I make at the clinic. I pay fifty percent of my income for state, federal and local taxes. I have adopted three children that I am raising. I helped pay for my sister to go to college. About twenty percent of the people we treat at the clinic cannot and don't pay. I give you four or five percent. This leaves me with about twenty-five percent to take care of my family. I hope you do not think that is too much.

If you still think you do not get enough I will tell you what you can do. Whatever money you can get off the people who do not pay at the clinic, you can keep for yourself. You are free to ask Kathy to give you the money I gave her to go to school. You can talk to Carol and see if she can make any savings on running our household. You would be welcome to that. If you can convince the govern-ment at any level to cut my taxes you are welcome to that as well.

Just think pastor how lucky you are. You work out of this church. I work out of the clinic. We are both in the business of helping people. Would you agree to that? Well, I have to pay property tax. You do not. What do you think the tax on this church would run? When someone comes to work for me in addition to paying them a salary we have to make payroll deductions. They pay social security and we have to match that amount for them. Then there is workman's comp, health insurance and federal and state income taxes. When we review their performances at the end of the year to decide on how much pay raise they deserve, you can not help but think that for every dollar more they have earned, some part of government is getting as much as they do."

Finally Jimmy said, "Father, these are all the things that I have taken into consideration when figuring out how much to give the church."

The pastor just looked at him in dismay. No one had ever talked to him like this before.

"Jimmy, why in the hell did you become a Catholic?"

The pastor had not heard a word that he had said. He did do one thing. He did what most people had been unable to do. He got Jimmy pissed off.

Jimmy said he sure as hell did not become a Catholic because of him.

"I'm glad, however, that we have had this chance to talk. I'm going to give you just one warning. Some young boys have come to my office in the recent past with what we shall say troubling stories or injuries. It's just a matter of time until one of them cracks wide open. When that happens your assistant will be in deep shit up to his deep neck."

With a sarcastic look on his face and the tone in his voice he said, "Well, Mr. Willow, is that all?"

"No, it's not. To you it's Dr. Willow and a good day to you if you ever have such a thing."

On his way home he couldn't think of anyone else who was more out of touch and a bigger ass than the man he had just talked to. There was not another Catholic church in a reasonable distance from where they lived. He decided not to tell Carol about his meeting, at least not now.

Two weeks later the assistant pastor was transferred out of the parish. Jimmy called the church to talk to the pastor.

"I see that your assistant has left the parish. I hope you got him some help and didn't just push him off on some other parish." There was no answer. The phone just went dead.

Over the next few days, although Jimmy had forgotten what Kathy said about the mayor she had been working on her assignment. Some time ago a lady came to visit her at the clinic. She was having female problems. Carol told her that one of the things that could be causing this problem was unclean sex.

The lady said, "You would think the mayor of this town would keep his dick clean."

Kathy remembered her visit. She knew the lady was single and she lived right across the street from the mayor. She also knew she worked at the super market. Kathy made several trips there and not just for shopping. She talked to this lady. After three visits she convinced her to come into the clinic. She told her she didn't look good and that she should come in for a check-up.

When she came to the office Kathy checked her over from head to foot. She was in top shape. Kathy told her she had gonorrhea and would need a shot. She was also told that since this was a small county the clinic worked closely with the health department. She would have to answer a few questions.

"Who have you had sex with?'

She named the mayor. She was told to go home and carry on her life like normal but not to have sex for one month.

When she left the office she was mad. Kathy knew where she was going. She gave her time to get there, then she called the mayor. He had already gotten the word. Kathy told the mayor that he had to come to the clinic and be tested. He sounded angry but said that he would be right over.

When the mayor came he was mad as hell. They put him ahead of the other people. He said, "I want to know what the hell is going on here."

Kathy said, "Look mayor, all we do here is test people and give them medication that will help them."

"Then tell me how in the hell I am supposed to have gonorrhea?"

"Mayor, all we do is treat people. You know how you got gonorrhea. Now do you want to be helped or not?"

"Of course I do."

What Kathy didn't tell the mayor was that her intercom had been left on and their conversation had been heard all over the clinic.

Jimmy was in his office when the mayor came in. He heard what came over the sound system. He laughed so hard that he had to get a glass of water.

Soon the word was all over town. The mayor had VD. The man he was running against had signs made up with this key message. Vote Down the mayor. The letters V and D being very large. The mayor was not only voted down but soon after the election, he left town.

With their new level of spending they were still not reaching the levels they felt were satisfactory. No one just wanted to give money away. They wanted some good to come of it.

Kathy had a beautiful baby girl. She was back at work at the clinic and would be taking over its management. This would give Jimmy a little time to spend on the trust.

What they had in mind was to be their ace in the hole. They had felt for some time that if they used the money to the level that the trust was earning, they would have to give it away. They would use it for medical research. They had no intention of getting into the research business themselves. Their role would be to fund other research for on going projects.

They soon found out that even some of the better recognized funds took a large percentage off the top for fund raising, etc. They needed some ground rules. First, they wouldn't give any money that did not go in total to medical research. Second, they wanted the research to be for children. It had to be something that would improve the lives of children. They didn't want it to be a plane ride to some fun spot for a child who had the kiss of death on him. This was a good thing but they wanted the money to work on the kiss of death. Third, it had to be for something of major importance. They would prefer that they work on something that would help most children not just a handful.

This was to be Jimmy's project. In the years to come he would spend many hours reviewing data on organizations and research work to try to make the best decisions. Many factors would go into his decisions. Some work was well funded by other organizations or the government. Some projects had come to dead ends years ago but were still being funded.

Jimmy had some ideas and he was looking forward to working on them.

Late one Friday afternoon, Jimmy got a call at the clinic. He thought he recognized the voice on the phone but he knew he had not heard it before. The man on the phone said, "Well, Dr. Johnny Thompson, I finally get to talk with you." Jimmy was wondering who the hell this was. He thought maybe Harry was playing a joke on him.

Then the man said, "You never called after you got the package. I am your cousin and the other half of the trust."

Jimmy knew his name and said, "Ben, where are you?"

Ben answered, "I'm sitting across the street from your clinic calling from my car. I know how you want to stay private and I would never do anything to change that, but I just had an over powering urge to see my only living relative. Can I come over?"

"Sure."

Most everyone had gone for the day when Ben was brought into his office. Jimmy noticed that he walked with a slight limp. He was about his size but he looked a little older. Compared together, Jimmy and Ben had a family resemblance. Ben was an inch or two shorter than Jimmy. His hair was starting to turn grey at the temples. The glasses he wore on his nose made him look like a college professor. Ben's shoulders were not as broad as Jimmy's but he was wider in the butt. This was probably because of his injury and his occupation. Ben's dress was noticeable both for its time frame and its cost. You might have called it "expensive hippie."

Jimmy thanked Ben for sending the box of items. Ben apologized for coming without notice. He just wanted to meet him and say hello. He had always wondered how Jimmy had turned out and what all that money had done to or for him.

Jimmy thought about telling him about the trust but wanted to hear more about him, first. He asked Ben to give him a run down about his life.

"Well," Ben went on. "I'm not proud to say but I was a wise ass growing up." He was a young kid in a rich family who always seemed to have better things to do than worry about him. He had some minor problems when he was young but nothing really bad. When he was eighteen he ran away from home and joined the army. He made it there just in time to get into the last stages of the Far East war. He was in the capital when it was over run. He was at the U.S.Embassy when he got wounded. He was airlifted out of the Embassy with some of the last to leave. He was in an army hospital for over a year. The limp he had now would be his for the remainder of his life.

His stay in the army lasted for three years. During that time his folks never contacted him. Neither did he contact them. When he was discharged he went to see them. He was still using a cane to get around. Although it had been three years, he had aged more like fifteen.

For the first time he took a hard look at how his parents lived. He felt it was good that he was an only child. Their only child was coming home from a war. He was wounded badly. He had earned a bronze star and a purple heart. He had been in a hospital for a year. Still he felt like he needed an appointment to see his own mother and father. If this was what big money did to people he was sure he didn't want any part of it.

They asked how he was but you could tell that they really didn't care. He was only with them about ten minutes. As he was leaving he told his father that he wanted to get a good education. He asked him if he would help. He said, "Sure, call my office in the morning. My secretary will take care of you."

Being unable to work at the time he enrolled in school. He needed help. His father's secretary took care of his school expenses and provided him with a small living allowance. He was being paid a little by the army for his wounds and he applied for the G.I. bill. This gave him some pocket money.

After he got into school he discovered he liked it. He went on to get his masters degree and full doctorate. For the past several years he had been a full professor of law. He said he liked teaching law but he didn't think he would like to practice it. He liked working with young people.

Ben went on to say that his mother and father died several years ago. Jimmy said that he had heard about his father giving money for a wing at the college hospital where he had gone. Ben said he knew about that. Ben mentioned that he went to his parents grave a few years after they passed on. He said all he could think of was what a waste.

"By the way. The estate that your parents left went to my father. I had never thought about that until now."

"Neither did I," Jimmy said.

"My parents left me some money. It was small compared to the total they had. Most of what they had was given to the arts. What they left me was enough to buy a nice home, invest a little and to be able to live nicely on a professor's salary.

Jimmy asked him if he was ever married?

Ben said that he had been married for a few years. It had been a mistake. He had gotten married right after his parents died. The girl thought he was getting alot of money. As it turns out that's why she married him. When most of his parent's money went elsewhere so did she. Ben said that was the only good thing his parents did for him and they never knew it. They helped him get rid of a money sucking wife.

He had never told her about the trust. A few years later after his ex-wife found out about it in the news she looked him up and wanted to get back together. When that failed she sued him stating that she had been cheated in the divorce. She was putting on a pretty good case until his lawyer asked her the name of her present husband.

Jimmy asked Ben what he had done with the trust money? He said, "nothing. Not a dam thing." He had all he wanted. He liked his life. He liked teaching and helping kids learn. He said that he had seen what all that money had done to his parents. They may have enjoyed life some but he doubted it. After they were gone he couldn't think of one thing they had done to help anyone or anything. He did not want that to happen to him. He wasn't looking at big things but he knew he had made a difference for some people. He said that maybe as he got older and hopefully wiser, he might have a use for the money. He had no one to leave it to.

They had talked for some time. It was almost six p.m. Jimmy had enjoyed his visit. He invited him to stay the weekend at his home. Ben thought for awhile and then said he would like that. What he had been thinking about was what Jimmy was going to tell his family about him. He mentioned that to him. They decided he would say he was a friend whom he had met in college. Everything else could be the same. Thompson was a common enough name.

Ben left his car at the clinic and went with Jimmy.

On the way to the farm Ben told Jimmy not to worry. He assured him that no one would find out about him from him. Jimmy thanked him as they drove up to the house.

That evening Ben fit right in with the family. He and Carol hit it off great. He played with the twins until it was bed time. When Carol was in the kitchen Ben asked Jimmy how old the twins were. He told them and added that they were adopted as well as the boy. Ben said they were great kids. He leaned over to Jimmy and said that they were the last of their kind. Jimmy nodded.

Later, Jimmy, without Ben's knowing, called Bob and Harry and made arrangements for them to meet with them the next morning.

When they got in the car to go to the office Ben asked Jimmy what they were going to do. He said he wanted him to meet his father-in-law and brother-in-law while he was in town. Hilda had breakfast for them when they got there. Jimmy introduced Ben. This time, not as a friend, but who he really was.

Bob asked him how he found out where and who Jimmy was. Ben said that several years ago he hired some-one to find him. He obtained his name and address but decided if he wanted to be private, so be it. Then, a couple weeks ago, he changed his mind. However, he had lost the name and address. He called the detective he had hired before he had moved. Then, just a few days ago, he was going through some papers on his desk and found it again.

Bob said that was before the changes he made. He hoped that if someone did that again with the changes he had made, they would be unsuccessful.

Jimmy asked Ben to help them when he went home. He asked if he would hire someone to try and find him again. He agreed. He said he would let them know if he was able to locate him.

Jimmy asked Bob and Harry to bring Ben up to date on what they had been doing with the trust funds. Ben showed an interest in hearing what they had done. He asked several questions. When they were done Ben said to Jimmy, "I cannot believe all that you have done with the trust. It's really great!"

Dr. Rhodes had arrived and had been present for most of their meeting. He asked Ben what he had done with his money. He told him what he had told Jimmy. The doctor simply said, "That's too bad." It was obvious that his comment cut deep into Ben. As he was leaving he said, "You know, doctor, not doing anything with that money is not very good is it?"

Jimmy drove Ben back to his car. Ben said he was glad that he had come. He told Jimmy he should feel lucky for the family he had. Jimmy said he thanked God everyday. He thanked Ben for coming and told him to feel free to visit anytime.

The day after Ben left they got a call at home from Hilda. She told Jimmy to go to Carol's father's house. He had taken ill and was in a bad way. Jimmy and Carol headed for the farm. When they arrived her father was in bed. Kathy was already there and she motioned for them to go into the bedroom.

Her father must have had a massive heart attack during the night. Her brother noticed he was not up in the morning for breakfast and found him. He was still alive and alert but Kathy told them he wouldn't be that way much longer. Carol knelt down at the head of his bed and took his hand. A slight smile of recognition crossed his face. He whispered he loved her. He said he had made it. He had lived long enough to see her happily married and to have her brother ready to take over the farm. He said now he was going to do something he had wanted to do for some time. He was going to be with her mother. The grip on her hand had eased. His eyes went blank and he was gone.

The funeral was hard on Carol. Her father had been like a rock all of her life. She kept thinking over and over what he had said. She knew he was in a better place. Jimmy had gotten to know Carol's father well. When he thought of an honest person he always thought of him. He felt that today the world had lost a good person and was just a little worse for it.

A few weeks after the funeral Jimmy had Bob look into the estate of Carol and her brother. It appeared that there was a will that left the farm to both of them. Bob arranged a meeting with them to explain what all that meant.

Carol and Jimmy wanted her brother to have the farm just like her father had intended. She only wanted a few odds and ends out of the house as momentos. Things were agreed upon between them. Bob followed through with the necessary paperwork. Her brother was very thankful for the help.

One day, out of the blue, the natural mother of the twins came into the clinic. She looked many years older than her age. She insisted on talking to Jimmy. He could hardly recognize her, at first. He had no idea where she had been all those years but time had not treated her well. He could tell she had been on drugs for some time and she seemed high when she came in. She was dressed like a hooker and if she was hooking it was in the poor part of town. She seemed unsteady and he felt she was there for medical purposes. He felt she probably had aids.

Upon talking with her, he learned that she wasn't there for medical assistance. She wanted to put a hit on him. She said she knew he was a big shot doctor but she also knew that he had her twins. She had agreed to put them up for adoption but not to him. She said it would be easy to prove that the children were hers.

Jimmy asked her what she wanted. She said she wanted money. He asked how much? She said she needed five thousand dollars a month. He said that was pretty steep. Reaching in his pocket, he handed her five hundred dollars saying that would help her for now. He would have to talk it over with his wife and she should come back tomorrow. She took the money and staggered out of the office. He wondered if she had understood what he had said. After she left he watched her as she made her way out of the building and into a waiting car. The man in the car looked as bad as she did.

At home that night he talked to Carol about what happened. They had Harry and Bob come to the farm and discussed it with them as well. They were coming up with all kinds of off the wall ideas. One plan was to have them arrested on drug charges. Another was to give them a large sum of money. and maybe she would just go away. All the talking got them nowhere.

The following morning Jimmy still didn't know what he was going to do. She was to show up at nine. He had held two appointments open for her. It was a little after nine and she had not shown. Jimmy decided to get a cup of coffee and read the newspaper while he waited.

On the front page of the newspaper there was a large picture of an auto crash. She and her friend had been killed. The article said that drugs had been suspected in the accident.

A couple days later in the paper Jimmy read that it had been drugs. He wondered if the money he had given her had been used to buy drugs. As no surprise to Jimmy, the paper said that both individuals in the car were in advanced stages of aids. For the rest of the day all he had in his mind was a picture of that young girl who he had helped several years ago.

# *Chapter Twenty*

Franklin had grown to be a nice size. It was now three times the size it was when they lived in the hollow. It was now the size town that had most of the services that improved life. It was small enough to avoid the coldness of the larger cities where most people didn't even know their next door neighbor. Here everyone knew and seemed to care for each other.

The town had taken over the dam that had been built up in the hollow. It was needed to supply water to the town.

The two extra corners at the highway interchange were now light industrial parks. The parks were less than half full but there were outfits still looking.

Kathy and Harry had sold their old house and had another one built on the side of the hill overlooking the town. They really liked their new place.

The little sports complex was being used for something almost everyday. It had become a focal point where the towns people got together. Parents and grandparents gathered there watching the youngsters play while visiting their friends.

Jimmy, Harry and Bob were talking about these and other things. They were having a Saturday morning meeting regarding the trust. They had started without Dr. Rhodes as he was late getting there. They had gone over some medical contributions they had made when Harry voiced his concern that the doctor was not there.

They called him at home but there was no answer. Jimmy said that he had not been looking well the last few weeks. He suggested that they had better go check on him. When they got to his house their worst fears were realized. It looked like the doctor had gotten up and dressed. He was fixing himself some breakfast when he died. He was lying on the kitchen floor.

Jimmy, like most, felt more like his father had died. He had been so close to the doctor. Upon hearing the news the whole town went into mourning. The amount of flowers and the size of the funeral was unprecedented for this town. He had done so much for so many people that no one else could hope to match him. Everyone was telling their favorite story about the doctor and how he had helped them in some way. He was truly a good man. The town was not only blessed that they had him but that he was able to spend so many years with them. The doctor was eighty-two years old. He had been active to the last.

It was like the town father had died. It took several weeks for the town to pick up and get back to normal.

Jimmy was sitting at his desk at the clinic. It was closing time. His car was being repaired so Carol came to pick him up. He said to Carol, "I would like to go over to the cemetery and visit the doctor on our way home."

When they got to the cemetery they walked over to

his grave. His head stone had already been installed. Someone had placed a bench at the foot of his grave. That seemed like a very thoughtful thing to do. You could tell by the ground that it was being used. They both sat there. Jimmy's mind wondered back over the years. He thought of all the things this man had done for him. He hated to think of what he might have ended up being if it had not been for Dr. Rhodes caring. He helped Bobby get into the academy. He helped Kathy get into school. He knew how many times he had helped Hilda. She had no money for their medical treatment but they always got the best. There were so many other things. It didn't seem that this grave alone should mark his passing. They both said a prayer and left.

On the way home Jimmy had an idea. He discussed it with Carol. He felt that they should have a statue of the doctor made. They should place it at the sports complex in his honor. Carol liked the idea. She said it would be good for the town, also.

Jimmy received a phone call from Ben. He asked if they were going to be at home that weekend. He wanted to come over for a visit. Jimmy told him to come over anytime, that they would be there.

On the way over Ben was in an accident. Actually, he had stopped for an accident and then, he was rear ended. It caused him to be a little later than he had planned. He arrived about eight p.m. Carol had already cleaned up after dinner when he arrived. She knew he was coming so she had saved him a plate.

After Ben took his things to his room he went to the kitchen for a late dinner. Jimmy poured himself a cup of coffee and joined him.

Ben told Jimmy about the accident he had on the drive over. He thanked Carol for being so thoughtful and for saving him something to eat.

Jimmy and Ben were alone in the kitchen when Ben told him there was something he had to talk to him about. That he was the only living person who knew what he was about to say.

Ben asked Jimmy if he remembered what he had said about his father? That he had gone to that medical school and told them that he would give them a million dollars for each year they kept him alive. Jimmy said he remembered.

"Well then, this is the rest of the story. On one of my father's mountain climbing trips or somewhere he got a rare blood disease. It was a slow kiss of death. With very close care they were able to keep him alive for a few more years.

One day out of the blue he gave me a call. We had not seen each other in over ten years. He didn't even call me when my mother died. He wanted to see me. I said, "What the hell for? You have not wanted to see me my whole life."

There was no answer. Then someone else got on the phone. It was a doctor who said that my father was dying. He only had a few days at best. If I cared to see him I should come quickly.

When I arrived he had a doctor and a nurse attending him at home. They took me right into his bedroom. He was alert. I sat on a chair by the head of his bed. He motioned for them to leave the room. He then began to talk. He looked very, very tired. He labored with every breath.

No matter how I felt about him I couldn't help but feel sorry for him at that moment. He said there was something he had to tell me before he died.

Years ago, he devised this plan. He set about to convince his cousin that they should set up a large trust with the bulk of the Thompson estate. They filled out and signed the paperwork. Then he encouraged his cousin to fly to Pittsburgh in the company plane. My father had a mountain climbing friend who was an expert on aircraft engines and explosives and at my father's instructions, this man rigged the plane to crash. The plane was to lose one engine about two hours out and the other fifteen minutes later.

"Are you aware that your parents were killed in that crash?"

Shortly after the crash my father found out that your father had already had the trust papers filed. He had killed five people for nothing.

His father's so called friend who helped him now wanted money. His father went on another mountain climbing trip with him and the friend never came back.

My father said he had grand plans for the money. How much money does one man want or need?

When I first heard about this I had no idea that you were alive. My father died shortly after our meeting. What was I to do? All the people who had anything to do with it were dead. There was no way to prove anything his father said was true if I wanted to.

All I could think of was that dam money. It must be true money is the root of all evil. This had just proved it."

Ben wanted nothing to do with the money. When that book about estates came out a few years back he hoped that one of the impostors would pull it off.

Like in Jimmy's case, he never contested their claims. He had never taken one cent from the trust. Because of what his father did he could not.

Because Jimmy was doing worthwhile things with the trust he felt he should give his part to him. Ben viewed it as cleaning up the money and doing some good things with it.

Jimmy didn't want anymore money. They were still having problems giving it away faster than it was building up.

Jimmy asked Ben, "Why now?"

"Because of your family and what you have done."

Jimmy thanked him for telling him the truth about what had happened. He knew Ben did not have a dam thing to do with it. He asked Ben to leave the money where it was for now. They could talk again at a later time. Ben had given Jimmy alot to think about.

In a couple of months the statue was ready. They

had it installed at the entrance of the complex.

The following Saturday they had a ceremony to dedicate it to the doctor. When it was unveiled one could see it was a very good likeness of him.

The inscription read, "WILLOW CREEK SPORTS PARK, IN MEMORY OF FRANKLIN'S MOST OUT-STANDING CITIZEN AND TOWN FATHER. MAY GOD BE TREATING HIM AS WELL NOW AS HE TREATED US WHEN WE NEEDED HIM."

A week after the statue was erected Jimmy went back to the cemetery by himself. He sat on the stone bench. He told the doctor about the dedication in the park. He thanked him for all that he had done. He told him he hoped he could be half the man he was. He lingered for awhile as if he was expecting an answer.

As he was leaving he noticed that there was one word carved into the stone on the back of the bench. FREEDOM. Jimmy had gotten his answer.

# *Chapter Twenty-One*

Well, that about completes the story. It has been a few years since Dr. Rhodes passed on. Kathy and I now have three children. Our oldest boy plays little league at the sports complex. We go there in the evening to watch and cheer him on.

Kathy has had the clinic running smooth now for several years. She loves her work. It doesn't seem possible that she is forty years old.

Jimmy puts his time in at the clinic but seems to rush home to Carol and the twins as soon as he can. Jimmy said, "You wouldn't know it. Most farmers say they are losing money." His farm had been making a nice profit." He would laugh when he was with the right group and say, "You just can't give the money away."

Carol was still a full time mom. She did it well and she loved it. The twins were seventeen and starting their last year in high school. Jimmy Jr. was twenty-seven and in his last year of internship. It looked like he would be joining the staff at the clinic.

Hilda was now sixty-five and still looking good. Bob was seventy-five and still in charge of the trust.

Mike married Miss Money from back east. They had two children and to everyone's surprise the couple was doing just fine. Mike was thirty-seven years old. He was the art director of a large museum back east. When he took the time to paint his paintings were selling for fifty thousand and up.

Jimmy's cousin Ben kept in touch over the years. He never re-married. He decided what to do with at least part of the money. He put a large amount of it into Jimmy's trust at the bank at Pittsburgh. He liked to laugh and say if Jimmy did not treat him right he would put more of it into the trust. He and Jimmy became close friends. He often visited and they both liked to fish.

You may have been wondering why I wrote this book. I have asked myself that several times. I was a late comer to this family. However, I learned something from each of them. I have often thought about Hilda. She was expecting at fifteen and had to drop out of school. By age twenty-one she had four children and enough abuse from her husband to last a lifetime. She a got a divorce and raised the children by herself. She never received a dollar of welfare. Not even one food stamp, not rent or electric money, no medical assistance. She did have help from friends. She would never take credit. She said that it was a team effort with her, Dr. Rhodes and Bob.

How did the children turn out? The oldest was a war hero who died for his country. Bobby got his fourth star and was in overall charge of the submarines and their development. Bobby was forty-eight and would retire in two years. He had agreed to replace Bob at running the trust when he did. Jimmy graduated at the top of his class at medical school. He was raising a beautiful family and spending his time his time at the clinic and with the trust.

Kathy was a doctor and she had a beautiful family as well.

Still why the book. "Well, I'm not a writer but a story teller. One evening at the sports complex two young boys were looking at the statue of Dr. Rhodes. One boy said to the other, "I wonder who that guy was?" One of those boys was mine. Right then, I knew if no one told them they would never know. I felt this story had to be told.

<u>The End</u>